Interludes

Interludes

a novel

by

Jared Walsh

SCAFFOLDS PRESS

PRINCETON

First Edition
Copyright 2019 by Jared Walsh

Manufactured in the United States of America

LCCN: 2017905610
ISBN: 9780692840719

"We shall define true happiness as the fond memory of true unhappiness."
—Bravo, *Meditations on Karmic Haine*

Chapter One

It will be boring to be dead, Lupo Bravo wrote his daughter, but at least I will shuffle through the underworld knowing I have left an echo on the surface. I do not mean in my writings, which are little more than the cave crappings of a misanthropic old hoot, I mean in you.

They told me, the doctors, the men of science—whom I continue to distrust, for they seem to know nothing but the hour of your death, and they cannot even tell you that—they told me that I had a hole in my heart, across which the electricity of life should not have the right to arc, yet does. Then they purported to show it to me. The hole shines like a silver stain on the image, it looks like a tyrestone earring hung on the heart's lobe. In linear form, on the readout of heart-signals, the hole represents an urgent whipping of the wings, a gust of offshore breeze come over the top of the wave crest. Death is prepossessing, in its way, when you notice that it dwells inside of you.

The doctors asked me if I wanted a "new heart." That was a difficult question, for I have always felt as if someone else's heart were lodged in my chest, and I was spending all my time trying to put the singing bird back in its rightful cage, or free it from its strictures entirely. But all the likely candidates for exchange were already dead, including freedom, freedom was dead. The voice in me has always been a bit foreign, has always spoken in a tongue that I feel I was not meant to understand. It has been uncomfortable: I will wake in the middle of the night, or be floored in the middle of the day, with some message from inner space, as it were, to record, for no reason. You must have the same predicament, if my estimation of your spirit still holds, if you have not squandered yourself somehow, and your message must also come not in known symbols and not in monochrome but in shapes with myriad facets and of limitless shades, a sort of diamond-delivery at all hours. It must be dreadful. It must be glorious too.

I told the doctors that I would not exchange this broken heart for anything, and that the gods can come find me if they are so greedy for my life.

I know I do not deserve to see you, I do not deserve to live my last moments with you at my side. I treated you horribly. I could not bear that you would suffer yourself to be made a common woman, that you would surrender your greatest gift, your mind, to the demands and the dreadful routines of a common man. I suspect that your life has not been quite so simple, and I suspect that you have not surrendered your temple at all, though there be vandals parading in the plaza outside, I suspect you have defied my sullen predictions, and that by your presence I will be humbled, and blessed still.

Take this watch, please, and return it to me before its motion runs aground. I have wound it only to the extent of three or four days' time, the most I can imagine waiting here on earth.

Chapter Two

Time touches down on the runway of consciousness. Mirra minds the gift of the watch and letter in the last tremble of her sleep. She steals away from the breast of Aden Pearlhorn and feels her way down the stairway to his study and makes herself another gift, of Pearlhorn's revolver. The revolver feels so alive in her hands, she imagines it could be set loose in the room on its own and make havoc, like a rodent taken foolishly as a pet. Her fingers vibrate over the surface of the barrel. Looking down the cylinder she can see that the thing is stuffed full of bullets.

"Chamber of chaos, so quiet," she says to no one.

She leaves in the ronewood gun case a letter knife and a paperweight, and brings the lock true. She laughs at herself: it is a childish ruse to play on her lover: he will not weigh the case without opening it. And he will not fail to find another means of playing his vain game on the lawn (where, she observed, smoking on the terrace the night before, ten antique mirrors lay shattered and warped), but before he goes hunting for another weapon to degrade his image, he will think of me and perhaps not do it at all. Mirra folds the revolver into her scarf and walks through the front gallery, into the central hall.

Enter Aden Pearlhorn himself, at the top of the main stairway. He capes then uncapes his body in an alcove, watching Mirra go. Pearlhorn reaches for her, he begins to descend without knowing it; he slips on a numis stair and hangs like a deposed monarch from the banister. Down just past Pearlhorn's throat there perches a sorrow, one that he cannot dig out, like a cacophone in a cage.

Further down inside Pearlhorn, past his vocal violins and next to his first memories (streams turning stones to trees), there dwelled the Mirra that did not leave, and this private Mirra and the private Pearlhorn hung at the same level in his own private sky, they equiposed on the surface of their own private morning.

Mirra did go, she went as always, she blinded and battered herself with the night of the foredawn. Pearlhorn lay down again on his bed and felt her rise from him a thousand times as the sun rose over his sills.

"No more of this," he whispered.

Chapter Three

Mirra made her half waking way back home. It was far down the decline to her cottage, where she seemed, to all others and even to those involved, to live with her family. In the cottage as she approached, there slept two Peters, one her son, and the other the son's father. Peter Senior drank deeply and slept with blinders on, to keep out the glow of the clock, or the television, as most times he went comatose in his chair. He never saw Mirra awaken next to him, and rarely did she. Bakeries bake early, and Mirra manned hers as punctually as woman may best. This had been the idea for ten years now. Mirra crept through the back door, showered, changed, nearly fell down the stairs, and crept into her Ayuda and onto the main road that leads to the village of Two Trees.

Past Mirra, so deep down in Pearlhorn that her harpists' fingers had his roots for lightstrings, dwelt Katherine Godwin, the image of perfection blurred into itself, and that perfection furled and unfurled forever, such that they, Godwin and perfection, spread fever in Pearlhorn's core. Godwin was too pure in appearance to be set off against the daylight with any specificity. She was half Mirra's age, the same as Mirra's son. At that moment, Godwin played with the leaves of a palm in an octagonal cupola encased in fog—her mother's studio. She boldened herself on visions of the nearby grove of trees burning, its ashes blinded the sun, they were the fog.

It was late late, too late. Mirra cried in the bathroom of her bakery. It was not so difficult for her to cry, she had years of practice. She cried for Pearlhorn, because he had whittled her down to soul, and there was no way left to operate except as a figurine of a woman for his toying-with. She had no voice left, it seemed, only a music she herself could not make out, a music the two of them could communicate but not decipher. This was bad for the both of them.

Mirra's son, just finding life again after a dream of a monstrous semaphore that would not turn green, lay in his bed and reached for the ceiling fan and turned it like a clock in his mind, it did turn. He turned it the other way. This was the thrill of art. His father, fetid, fumed in the bed and spilled ashes on the carpet. (Godwin daydreamed of Mirra in a glass elevator atop a striped horse. The dream did not end well—the animal took flight and defied the glass but not the ground—better for me, because it is harder to write a dream that does.)

Mirra flown, and his coffee made and brought by Ianthe, the maid, Pearlhorn started packing a bag. He did not wonder for where. Every school year's end he flew away to Santa Theresa, an island nearer the maximum of the Earth's girth, where he could be alone, or close to it. This year he was traveling with

Etienne Opienne, his childhood and later schoolhood and manhood friend in letters, and, less and less (to Opienne's chagrin), lechery. This last thing Pearlhorn had renounced so many times, the machinery of renunciation was beginning to break down (whereas Opienne's machinery of renunciation renunciation was well-oiled and running strong as ever). Pearlhorn started packing a bag, but he did not put anything in it. He called for Ianthe, who was already in the doorway with his second cup of coffee, and fucked her graphically but efficiently. Then Ianthe packed the bag.

Mirra cried still in the bathroom and reached inside herself philosophically and tried to dig out Pearlhorn. It did not end well. She could not do it. Her body had a shiver of brute sickness, as if her organs had been whipped and twice-baked in her skin. Is this what is meant by love?

Chapter Four

We are in Two Trees, a town between two cities, one more histor-
ically important and the other better known. We are landlocked
with Pearlhorn, with the Peters, with Mirra, with Godwin, with
Scarlet. Lupo is not landlocked but skylocked and sealocked.
Everybody seems to be boozelocked. It is surely this time, this
go-around, because my chest is a hollow drum, he thought, that
I will die. The light married then parsed the sky and sea. Lupo
rose. He stood over the sink and coughed for about an hour. He
took a drink of wine.

In that landlocked place where the parsing of day and night
was puzzled by treetops, Mirra bucked up, as it were, and baked,
and brewed, and busied herself with steel wool about the stove,
which was showing a mysterious stain that she could not scrub
free. Her first patron was revealed. By gods it was Pearlhorn.

He had come, as he had come so many times, to tell Mirra
that he could no longer see her—that he was of impure heart
and impulses (Ianthe), that he was freakishly undeserving of her
(Ianthe &c.)—that the affair was becoming too much of a marriage, and marriages could only end in disaster (his parents had
been screaming at each other when they were killed, screaming

over nothing, screaming was better than nothing, at that point). But then Pearlhorn gave one hard on Mirra's lips, and he felt it, then, still. Despite being his (and he loathed anything and anyone that would suffer itself or herself to be possessed by him, despicable him), Mirra was superior to all but the pagan host in the salacity and sagacity of her body and mind—and even above the gods, for the melt of her thoughts into the bright mold of her features could be seen, and touched.

"I have a question," he said.

"I think I know what it is."

"You may not know."

"Then make me know."

"Come to me, leave your family, do not be apart from me anymore, be my . . . you know."

He kissed her again, and he felt it, she was crying, she could cry indeed, she was losing her footing, she was losing her constitution. He wiped her eyes with his lapel, and the glisten stayed there, for a moment.

"Wife is scullery, Aden. Mistress is queen. What will I be now?"

"You will be someone who finds herself a more original definition."

"Once we go away, we will have to stay away."

"Santa Theresa."

"Just I need until Saturday."

"I teach until Friday, as you know. So I was planning on Saturday."

"You. Were not planning anything. You thought this up in the doorway on the way in. But I need to visit my father, my father is dying."

"Terrible. Where?"

"What does it matter where a man dies?"

"What if he doesn't die?"

"Don't get hung up on nonsense."

"Etienne will be coming too."

"Less than perfect. He is a goat of a man."

"And what of your goat of a husband?"

"   . . .   "

"   . . .   "

An actual patron entered, ordered, received, paid, sneezed, and left.

"I don't care about him, Aden. Focus, focus. What do you really need to do?"

"Call the pilot."

"No, Aden. You probably already called the pilot. You need to say your goodbyes."

Aden leaned in again, then he blew away in the street. Loudly. His car was an Annapurna, so rare they don't exist.

Upon touching his third cup of coffee to his lips, knee to the wheel and free hand to the ronewood shifter, Pearlhorn thought of his good-byes. The thought gave rise to a vibrant and stultifying tingling in the legs. He pulled an erratic u-turn in the street, barely missing two identical young women out with their babies, or someone else's babies, for an early morning stroll, and dodged through his estate's "town" entrance, a pair of stone columns capped with cartoon gargoyles, for an actual drink. The wine botched all his train cars and reordered them properly, in echelon formation. He looked from within the terrace doors. His view was not Lupo's, but it was fecund, and higher for sure. The parsing of morning confused and corrugated by treetops, and baffled by the murdered mirrors that lay about on the grass.

Ianthe arrived with a fourth cup of coffee. Aden waved her off. She was not pleased. Then he followed her into her room and fucked her again. In the restive stained light of her pillow, while she wiped herself and smelled the napkin and made a goblin face, he thought,

Uselessness . . . Mirra . . . Santa Theresa . . . Good-byes. And what of Godwin? He had not been thinking so much about Godwin before, in fact had forgotten she existed—this would happen to him, with women and girls—the women occupied one sphere, the girls the other, as savories and sweets. Godwin did not qualify as a good-bye: she had not yet crossed his threshold. And to Pearlhorn's limited knowledge of the future, if Godwin did not cross that threshold soon, he would have to catch up with Godwin in a few years, when Godwin's charms were wasted and his own had weakened considerably, and Mirra was, say, laid up with fever. Add to this, Godwin's crossing was unlikely to unfold at all. In his office this week, the last week of high school, after which all ropes were down, Katherine Godwin, that image of perfection, had thanked Aden for his letter of praise—it had lubricated her way into the University of Ex, my employer, whose spires and seers elevated the city of Tarne—but laughed off his invitation to dinner on Friday with Ex's most debauched poet, author of *Letters to a Flute* and *Sick My Assonance.*

"I don't enjoy Opienne. He tries too hard."

"How about Pearlhorn? Do you enjoy him?"

She laughed again, but this time directly at him as a man, a poet, and everything. His neck met his niff. Nonetheless, he had to have her at least once, no less than he had to have Ianthe, the maid, at least twice a day. Ianthe approached again, for a third time, from across the pillow. He waved her off, begging the fact that his guts were beginning to turn flaccid. She cursed him, beautifully, in German then in Swiss German. I must find a second tack through this strait: I must wind a clock, he thought, and Godwin will come to me, like the night. But then, how to say good-bye to the night? How very typically hopeless of me. (Aden was a poet and a drunk, and therefore something of a believer in the impossible. Not such a believer as I, but still a believer.)

He needed a second tack, because the third and final tack through the straits of uselessness was self-annihilation, and Pearlhorn was already self-annihilating at a flying pace.

Pearlhorn drank again, and he reached the bottom of the bottle. He hoped another bottle was nearby, found one at the bedside, smelled it. Many others were downstairs in a cellar, but going there meant finding hooting apparitions of the dead: his father's ancient cigarettes burdened the crenellated ashtray, and his mother's scarf showing dour treppan imprint woven through with carmine jazz mazes still wept over the back of a sipping-chair. Candles burned over Queen's Bender, their favorite card game, still wept there too. He did not go into the wine cellar, the maid did. Ianthe. And so did Mirra.

Lupo was not so shy about his wine. He made account each morning of the casks that kept his stores, not for fear of loss but for fear of thirst. He did this this morning, despite his decrepitude. He took another drink, his third, we missed his second, I apologize, I am in a strange mood. Then he counted the coffee trees that hovered in the shades they made, and walked to the very brim of the world, and slow, couched by waters, his heart swinging like an axe against his chest. I want her here, to know she is alive, said Lupo to himself, and I believe she will come. The belief, and even the feeling that it was against reason and probability, warmed him.

Peter Lynch Senior knelt beside the toilet and perpetrated a reversal of fortune for yesterday's nourishment. Lynch's son, Mirra's son, lay low in the shades that were just acquiring limits. A dark one shone over him, she shone fine night against undefined. Not Godwin—not this moment. Not quite Scarlet. And not yet Mirra. Mirra is the end. Do not rush me.

Chapter Five

Lo unico pecado . . . Lupo said to himself. He stood on the beach. He scraped the edge of the world's canvas with his eye's fingernail. Hues, was all, and ever would be, sand, and hues, and a viola whose player never materialized. Mirra was that mysterious musician, she was named after the image that was not there, the only one one knew. He scraped further along the horizon. Its centerpoint rose, the other parts fell, the horizon is a wave, the horizon is an iris. He was almost glad the burn mark was so direly carved into his heart. Almost. The inimitable, the coy lashes of the sea against the land . . . I will meet Mirra in the afterlife, perhaps, and she will pick up her instrument and play for me, as I imagined it before she was conceived. But there will be so many others about, and I will not find her. Might as well live a moment longer.

Chapter Six

Pearlhorn walked down the hall of Marywood School. Kill me today, or some time tomorrow, he said to himself, off me so that I do not cause any more pain. I am losing sense of time, because my internal metronome pauses for longer and longer to catch its breath, and in that pause all time is swallowed. He walked further down the Marywood hall. Death to me, the death sentence, I should utter, he thought, and that way draw her to me, plant a seed of urgency upon this algal sea of waste. But then how continue, how retract? I cannot retract. It must be some happenstance fissure in things that keeps me from the grave. And she will see straight through the ruse, the suicide. She does not care, Godwin is lost to the gods, she knows that death comes to all, and still she does not move on it. I am too drunk still. It is always this way with me. A kelping of my whole life, such that it, with the rest of the universe, and my verses too, sink into the bottle and suffocate there. My beginning is where most people end: utter wastedness. Who rises from all this, who is my Phoenix and Perdix?

Pearlhorn fell, so it felt, into his classroom. His, because he was its magisterial polestar. He began to see who else was there. There was Godwin. There was Peter Junior. There was Scarlet May. There were more, but they didn't matter. He sat down at his desk, gingerly, pretended to look for some papers in his satchel, and finding papers there full of naught but his inscrutable thoughts on Fabian Loome, comedic novelist of *In My Tumbler* fame, he stood as best he could, and began:

"I begin with a digression. You know, you all know, about this war going on, between light and dark, diaphanous and cloudy, fulsome and banal, transcendent and material. And you may sense, from my lectures and meanderings, that my . . . spirit prefers the light, although it rarely possesses the strength to reach it. Nor do I believe that any of the literary characters we study, even God himself, have the strength to be immune from their surroundings (thus the banishment of Satan). That is crudely put, I know. But I do find that my . . . constitution requires an exile from all this interplay of . . . this and that . . . in the thoughts of man, a voluntary exile abroad, a self-banishment, to a place where none can reach me but myself. At the end of this week, I will take refuge for an indeterminate time nearer the center belt of the Earth, and outside the jurisdiction of this mad hatter of a state of mind. So, fare thee well, you have been a wonderful and patient and rightfully challenging group of individuals, and I wish you all the numis stones of such wisdom as you can find by the side of these paths, or in the canyons of your minds, if there you do dare go . . . Now the lesson."

The scene developed. The cluster of heads began to nod, to write, to nod off. The sound of feverish rackbirds approached the windows, bounced about in the classroom, and fled to the coast. The air became thick with thought. Pearlhorn kept his eye to his (imaginary) notes, but then he did not keep them there, and they boarded the train to Beauty and back—first to the country scene on the far wall, a child's mother watching her water an amaranth grove; thence to Scarlet before one arrived with incurable momentum at Godwin, and paralysis. He noticed that his scheme, little more than the announcement of the immediate truth with a thin tail of embellishment, had worked profoundly upon the girl's features.

"He will not go away without me," said Godwin to herself, behind her lips, but with a murmur of a movement in them, and she wrote it on a piece of paper that she passed to Scarlet May. Scarlet mouthed something back, the receipt of which caused a rain of what the portraitist might call flavor to precipitate down Godwin's body.

Chapter Seven

Mirra was halfway through the morning, a morning deflated by the bearing of witness to so many other humans who all seemed to be defective in some ghastly way. She jogged Lupo's watch from her pocket and peered at it. The face peered back at her.

The smile of the watch, sprinkled with childhood superstition, told her that Lupo breathed, but the halt of the second hand told her that his breathing was deliberate. She saw him in the foredawn before her arrival, the viola-notes of first light wriggled against the sky. (They both had an attachment to that instrument, the unsung heroine of the orchestra.) Inside of him, he has an igneous image of me that is cool and hard and prickish to the touch, breakable like a flake of subterranean fire just cooled. That image is drawn in the black of his violence, his violence in return for my defiance, that swift boxer's touch he gave my orbital bone, delivered near the beachy spot where he no doubt stands scraping the sky with his oracular eye. The vision of me brutalized by him must fix him still, in the hooks of a grimace so permanent that it has herded his features narrowly about the nose. The rest of him likewise must hunch down and crowd around his loping heart, as if deflated by a lightning blow from the skies. Poor man.

She replaced the watch in her pocket and went on working. It shocked her there, ghostly shock, throughout the rest of the day. It was the shock, she felt, of all the time she had wasted in response to that first boxer's touch. Eighteen years.

Eighteen years ago, Peter Lynch had been a carpenter in Lupo's employ for the impressionistic rectification of a wall of paneling in the study, an inconsistency of sheen that had bothered Lupo for some time. The paneling was not technically crooked, but it appeared crooked exactly at the moment when one tamped one's pipe into the fireplace, and peered to the side to be sure that one's head would not come to blows with the mantle. With some complication involving the poisoning of an innocent set of straight lines, Lynch rebuilt the paneling and replastered the wall, and while Lupo was out at Ex giving his history lectures (some of which I attended, as a graduate student, and later as a disciple and junior lecturer myself), Peter Lynch plastered and replastered, and eventually poisoned Lupo's daughter. There was an aborted abortion, hearing of which (from the Doctor whose appointment was missed) Lupo clocked his daughter and cast her loose. Eight months later, Peter Junior came into the world, a thin film coating his face.

When Peter Junior had made seven years, and Mirra had passed through at least as many phases of maternal and conjugal desperation, William "Wild Bill" Pearlhorn, owner of Two Trees' largest, eponymous, estate, on the grounds of which the Lynches occupied a generous gardener's cottage, died prematurely and monstrously while taking the Sunday breeze in his Peripatete with his wife, Noreande "Nore" Pearlhorn, who died beside her husband's crooked corpse. That week, Wild Bill and Nore's one son returned home from Ex, where he was giving and taking in equal measure a doctorate, under my tutelage, in English, Whitson, and Wine, and delivered two bold eulogies at the funerals, in which life was personified as a shepherdess orbiting a crystalline alpine lake, and receding, and losing focus, but never disappearing. At the reception, a thousand soul affair where tulamore flowers shipped on ice from the Enseen marshes floated in the punch bowls and the discarded carcasses of three dozen barn animals attracted an avenging galaxy of as many scavenging birds, Mirra wandered from the common rooms of the Two Trees mansion and into the maid's quarters. Pearlhorn lay there on the couch, under a stained glass window depicting the landing at Gonfleur, and he abruptly came to and closed and latched the door behind them and tilted a burgeoning champagne bottle into Mirra's mouth before she could tell him all the reasons why (she had assembled them during the shepherdess speeches) they should conduct a long, dark, clandestine love affair in which he consistently betrayed her with everyone he could find and she found a new set of rungs each week from which to drape her despair.

Chapter Eight

Peter Junior partook in equal portions of his father's vulgarity and his mother's madness. The thin film that divided the two was an oily skin of what he felt was genius, and perhaps on account of that very feeling he knew it was not yet. Peter knew his English, he knew his Greek, he was reaching for Latin, and he knew a good deal of Josfrende and Dooring and Lome and Timbersaand, but he did not feel powerful enough to put all that aside and begin something of his own: he was too beset with thoughts, forethoughts really, of what it was he ought to be thinking about. All this circularity drove him halfway ill at all hours, and if mirrors did not disabuse him of the notion, he would have drawn his self-portrait (if he could draw) halfway bent by his own confusion, his spine perfectly parallel with the ground, like that of a disgraced hero tarred and feathered and limping through the town, and moaning internal jeers. The vortex of Godwin gave Peter vertigo, Scarlet gave him cramps. Sequential auricular joggings (i.e. biradial cacophones) gave him chills. Laughter made him cover his face with his arm. Rich food and rich writing made him sleep, and sleep made him far more weary than he had been before. His weariness would hit an asymptote, fall into numbness, and swing back into confusion. Because he could not read for long before feeling the surfeit of the words, he treasured poetry over prose, and especially the listless or dim. *My apologies / your words failed to reach me / in the midst of the preachy / people that gathered, / not that it mattered.* Poetry over prose, and weariness mixed. His feathered hair was that way because he slept under a fan that made things flow so, to drown out, partly, the whirring of the cacophones in the darkness outside. His eyes were never satisfied with your plaints or plains or plans. His whole face was off just slightly to the one side, but imperceptibly. Scarlet May once called him beautiful. He reciprocated. They were seven.

"He will not go," says Godwin again. She is lying down and intermittently bouncing erect in the back seat of Peter's grandfather's very old station wagon. In the front, Peter and Scarlet pass back and forth a bottle of Old Bit, a malt liquor of which they have been finding drive-size specimens in the door linings and stash compartments of the station wagon for years, without fail (except when they could not find any more, and raided the door linings and stash compartments of Peter Senior's truck, with horrifying success). When the present bottle hovers in its most vulnerable state of transit, Godwin snatches at it from her state of repose, and tilts it, from the side, at what seems to be a newly discovered angle, into her throat. In her other palm there slowly melts a chalky key to her release from the gyre Pearlhorn has put her in: Godwin has been raiding her mother's medicine cabinet, also with horrifying success, and also for years, except for the time her mother caught her raiding it, at which point Godwin started raiding the other caches, and her mother gave up and put everything back into the medicine cabinet. Godwin swallows the pill. By the time Peter pulls into her driveway, Godwin is in Innisfree, and the incline of the property's apron and the undulating idle of the engine fall into equilibrium: she hovers there, in Innisfree.

Chapter Nine

Lupo reached down about his sandal, groaning,

No hay mas que conocer.

(There is nothing left to know.)

In this crescent of sand that forms between my large and lesser toe, there is more to observe and to know—the quiver of daylight multiplied in the quiver of my heart's periodic tumescence, and in the million glances of all the sand's faces—than there could possibly be known by means of what they call learning, which is mere imitation of the thoughts of the dead.

Todo que podria conocer, pero no conozco, permanece.

(All that I might have known, but I do not know, remains.)

Chapter Ten

In the dusk, already five driving beers into the dusk, and having blasted up the Two Trees driveway hot and fit to drink more and lose consciousness in his chair, Lynch heard the furor of Harry, the last of the family cats, issue from beneath his front tire. Lynch waited in his seat for some time, a time that diminished in sweetness, for it approached the time when he would have to stop waiting. He got out and looked. The thing, for it was no longer a cat, coughed its last, of undifferentiated death. That last cough brought Lynch to disgusted tears. He had had issues with the cat, issues of personality, of habit, of space management, of excessive excretion, but none to justify murder.

He gave the corpse a small salute and an even smaller, but firm, gesture signifying good riddance, and he wrapped the phantom thing in a blanket and sent it into the sky from a firepit situated far down a forest path from the cottage and boled by tule and ungiflora and starspotted with crift. Tule is a tufted sentry of the upper space. Ungiflora is an evergreen claw that gnaws at the earth. Crift is our limitless audience, an olympic nenophar on the earthly lake. Toward things such as the burning corpse of the animal, and farcical men such as Lynch even, the cheeks of the crift flower turned, fat and splendid. Lynch vomited. The cat smoked unevenly. Lynch smoked too, to cut the ripeness of the air and the punge of his palate. Lines of last light, made hirsute by the floor of the forest and made crystal ornament by the smoke, framed him. Visions of plague in the melting animal cursed him. *A Decade Of Fire,* he misthought, knowing he did but knowing not how—it was the title of a book of poems that spent its Sundays sprawled on Mirra's heaving and withdrawing chest, on which the poor Harry, too, used to sprawl, and rise and fall with the breathing of Mirra. Mirra was a compulsive rereader—unlike their son—a half- and quarter-reader—and unlike Lynch himself, a non-reader—so Lynch ought to remember the name of her most treasured book. *The Time Of Smoke,* he misthought again, and he prayed, so far as a man can do, that the cat would melt more quickly, to spare Mirra the sadness and him the brilliantly crafted emotional beating when the cat did not. In life the animal had been a ruthless tyrant—it would not die; in death, its intransigence remained—it would not apotheosize.

(The title of the book was *Years, Their Embers,* by Whitson. It was my first book of poems, conceived when I was nineteen and published ten years later, once I had completed twenty-nine pieces that I thought I could live with. The result, to my eye, did not enrich anyone but the author; it was a formal exercise, a marionette dance of the pencil with marionette stars, an unlikely and unlucky, and ultimately clumsy coupling of lead with paper. I would have done better to let the number of poems correspond to the number of years I thought I had left, in lieu of those I had spent: I might then have held myself back forever, and on my last breath dropped a single golden strophe.)

Lynch prayed, too, that the cat would not melt and that Mirra would draw from the scene the most fantastical negative inference (that he had staged with the cat a tragicomic and now inexorable reenactment of the martyrdom of St. Sephasius, for example). Having made so many futile sacrifices in the name of what might be called soft monogamy, and having seen not a single one of his forays into connubial solicitude bear fruit, Lynch thought to trigger in Mirra's face that special rage that struck her resemblance to Dolce Rita, one of the table girls at the Socratian Casino. The Socratian Casino was where Lynch invested his savings, in hopes that one day he could afford himself enough cocaine to blow himself into the next century—in a room at the Socratian Casino.

What sort of god did Lynch invoke, in his prayers? Was it a proletarian beggar-god, a glutted Mammon, syphilitic Athena? Was it a priestly god, dysenteric Christ? Was it an animal god, bovine Jove? Was it the dispossessed Echo, the arachnine Shiva? At times like these, when his mistakes were involved, it seemed the entire Pantheon had assembled to cast aspersion on him, the Heavenly host too, little pale penises and brass trumpets erect, and the Stygian flotsam, Saturn in his dressing gown patched with the dripping hides of the howling millions. Assembled in the night sky as a multitudinous dreary halo illumining his sins in all the darknesses of the vengeful supernatural, the gods seethed in ten thousand unintelligible tongues, yet somehow they all glowered at him with identical black eyes, and indicted him with the same Spanish lips, as Mirra did as she approached him stoking the fire.

Chapter Eleven

Godwin starts. It is nearly dark again. She attempts to rise, her ardor bleeds out, she flops back down on the bed and with a numb hand picks at a spot of color in a bowl by the reading lamp. She sucks off the flesh of a sternfruit and pushes its almondine pit through her pucker, and the pit tumbles and bounces down her pillow and over the lip of her bed. She raises her brow at this messy accident (the sternfruit pit will leave an ink-blue stain in its trail that is impossible to expunge), and as she does, she feels herself forcing the expression for the benefit of an imaginary observer. As she wakes up in the mind, her consciousness occupies a set of subterranean mezzanines where familiar monsters socialize with one another, an executioner's convention. Let me not think, she whispers.

"Let me not think."

But she thinks.

Pearlhorn wastes in his study at home, and he thirsts. By design he has no drink here, only ghosts of poets and failed poets, one of whom is Pearlhorn. A poet is a failed poet until he dies; then, he is either a poet or no one.

Mirra's watercolor of the royal family of gods lies on Pearlhorn's desk, not far from the locked ronewood gun case, but far enough such that the perusing of the watercolor does not necessitate the kenning of the case. The painting is all he sees or can see. It depicts the entire ethereal household in graphic sexual and murderous labor and submission, their faces jocund or droll, simpering mad or effortlessly calm, their bodies hot flashes of earthly energy, and all of it vivid as if they had all posed for a photograph in those impossible poses. She would burn the work, Mirra had told him, or he could have it. Mirra was this way with her art: she would have burned this master-piece, as she did all of them, to feel the need for another rising in her mind. Pearlhorn imagines burning the painting himself, so as to equate himself, at least in destruction, with his idol. The thought plies out to the far reaches of his life, the ones that his mind can only indicate from afar, with its thinking-stick. Here is my ancestry, and here is the supination signaling its absence. There is my body, and flying from it, as so many freak leaves of autumn, my dreams. As if bled from those dreams' veins, this watercolor. He runs his finger along one of the girl's shocked lips. The little nymph is getting raped—laboriously, rapidly, and perfectly. A purpuline drop of blood hangs from her thigh. Pearlhorn cannot burn the painting, but he thirsts still for de-struction that will prompt renewal.

She thinks. Godwin thinks. I would like to proceed in the di-rection of night. It being nearly night, I will not miss the mark. But how shall I proceed then? How shall I, little I, proceed in anything? Night gives to day, I will seek the night and fail, I will seek the day and find myself thwarted by night. I want the earth to cease its useless motion, so that I might meditate on the final thing, the irreducible thing, and hold it inside of me. But why is it necessary always to want something? Do you not think you have that final thing? And what is it worth…once gotten? What will you then know? Come on Katherine. What will you then *know?*

Chapter Twelve

Mirra called for her son, who appeared at the foot of the stair. He embraced her, her body was soft and forgiving.

"Why are your hands dirty?"

"I buried Harry, or rather his charred corpse, with your father. Your father was cooking him."

"We are not that poor . . . I thought . . . that we needed to consume the cat."

"It was a cremation. Your father had killed him, not slaughtered him."

"Killed him. Maliciously?"

"By accident. Though it is difficult to run over a cat."

"What kind of accident?"

"A car accident, I guess. Or a truck accident."

"That man is a human accident."

"Your father is harmless. Just dull, and dull-witted."

"The two forces, harmlessness and idiocy, are at odds."

"I think you're wrong. One must have one's act together to do true harm."

"What is the difference between true harm and false harm?"

"Don't scrutinize my sayings. I'm tired. And in the space of fathers, my father sent me a note. He's dying. I'll go to him."

"It's late."

"You're right, it is late, almost too late. That is why I need to go."

"Can I meet him, at last?"

"You had better stay here. If you came, you would only lose more than you will already. Some day you will lose me. And death is not for the living."

Peter Junior lay once again under his fan and let his head fall sideways. He had almost loosed the dogs of his dreams into the familiar landscape (a receding horizon, a pair of houses far too close to one another, a paxwood in bloom, the long grass, the low rose sunlight scattered through stained glass skies) when Godwin called.

"You should still be comatose. We had to carry you upstairs."

"Hello Peter. I wonder something."

"I wonder many things, Katherine."

"Can I try something on you?"

"I am tired of things being tried on me."

"I swear it won't hurt. It will only hurt on the inside."

"I hate you so much that I love you."

Chapter Thirteen

In the tradition of Dooring, Lupo's arch-nemesis and a fat, famous philosopher poet who spooks the turning of these my first
few prose pages, I should say a word about Aden Pearlhorn's
mind. The defining feature of Pearlhorn's mind was its elusive-
ness. He began his days full of vacancy, so to speak, and the
mind, loosely defined as the organ charged with verifying Aden's
presence upon the earth, or at the very least his presence in his
body, would be nowhere to be found. So, if a mind firmly seated
in its body is a *person*, or *somebody*, Aden walked into the daylight
as a *nobody*, a *bloodless wound*. He expended the vast majority of
his diurnal efforts scratching at the laceration inside of him.
With labor, with drink, with lassitude and spectacular self-deri-
sion he destroyed layer after layer of spiritual epithelium, and
he lay down to rest at his most vulnerable, dejected, afraid, and
of course drunk. To this raw husk of a thing, or more properly
to this raw husk of a *nothing*, that remained, the mind returned
home, during sleep.

What had gone wrong?

In the much fabled before, Aden had been a devout wor-
shipper of himself. The basis of his faith had been his unlikely

survival despite daily crossings of conflagritous tarfields of loss. His parents' death had lain the molten macadam for him; all he had had to do, before, was to evade the sinkhole of suicide, and he became his own god, permitted to take up his pencil at any time and record even the most jejune offal of his imagination for the consumption of eternity. His mourning gave him *The Volant Fing, Starlight on Jupiter, Boon Songs.* It gave him the fortitude and desperation to sit for thousands of hours and to produce the epic *Holy Moss,* a poem he had considered from the start to be crapulous and vain. Then his mourning ran out, and sadness flown, there was nothing to take its place. He would not dream of seeking contentment, the swill of mediocrity, he would not become a poet of ennui, the darkness was his vehicle, his unattainable vehicle though ubiquitous. Would that his had been some sort of poet's block! His present condition was far worse than "not being able to write", it was the poet's worst ephialtes of life as a non-poet, and the nightmare was so meticulously crafted as to lack a single clue that the dreamer was dreaming.

Still sitting in his study, Aden reached for Mirra's watercolor again. He touched Persephone's hand. He made large eyes at the watercolor, he took his gaze away, and a verdiglow impression of the thing remained. All over his field of vision, the gods were having a hell of a time.

"Can I burn this verdiglow impression? Just as Mirra's burning of her paintings gives her that thimbleful of pain she needs to go on, I need something to destroy, I need a catastrophe, however small. But I am numb even to catastrophe."

Pearlhorn was so numb to catastrophe, numb to all other extremes of temperature that might otherwise have set him alight, that the resting heartbeat of his spirit was akin to the blind seethe of the constellations over the head of a fogged-in sailor in irons, he could not tell the difference between dying and why, truth and noose, piano and fandango, and in such an outer space of his inner space he could do anything, and therefore nothing.

One small advantage to Aden's self-distance was that the removal of his mind from its body rendered him never quite alone. Aden's mind hovered somewhere out there, for sure. Perhaps it sneered at him from the outstretched arms of the Redding's oak beyond the north windows of his study. Perhaps it gaped around the earth at him, from the Zephyrs. Perhaps it spent its time peering out at something else. But at times, Aden felt, he locked eyes with his mind in a sort of haters' romance.

Chapter Fourteen

"Quien soy? No me importa quien soy."

Lupo had stopped wondering who he was. He knew that he was, as opposed to wasn't, and soon would not be. Four days. Three days or four. Four is not exactly a number. The crucifix has four points, and it is the gateway to naught. Three days, then.

"Pero quien soy?"

Lupo was known by the world as a teacher and philosopher of history. His delightful analysis of karmic haine (*Meditations on Karmic Haine*), and his use of that theme to define the outer arc of human tragedy, was known to the Historical Society as the commanding monograph in the last thirty odd years dealing with what the Society called aboriginal strife. The Historical Society did not understand, or want to understand, what Lupo had meant by "karmic haine." Lupo's wife, Ekaterina, had claimed to know and understand him, before she forgot everything on account of the mental scimitar that killed her. The trees and vines, the umbrella of sky, could not know Lupo besides to say, if they could say . . .

From time to time a stroke of gratitude to the trees and vines, the parasol of sky, was played by Lupo on his violin, in accompaniment, he imagined, to Mirra's viola, whose player never materialized. Lupo's gratitude loosed itself from the upside down smile of the strings and wandered the night as a creature among creatures, the cacophones and night birds, the other bodiless voices—the sea.

Chapter Fifteen

What of Godwin's identity? Her father Roland was a barrister and a lost drunk, literally lost, for no one had seen him since the Ravelston Kooks won the World Championship. Her mother Dorothy was an artist and an addict. Godwin preferred sax to piano, but had tried neither. She had tried her mother's uppers, downers, sidewinders, and boyfriends. She did not wonder who she was, knew for certain who she was: she was Godwin, a dilettante—or, as she sometimes fashioned it, an aesthete—and she judged herself by what or whom she transformed or transfixed, more often addled or vexed utterly. Destroyed.

For example, let us spy for a moment on her and Peter. Having accepted her invitation to her experiment, having greeted mutely a half-naked Dorothy in her studio, Peter lay fully naked on Godwin's bedroom carpet. The room was blue darkness over white walls, and the grey darkness from outside poured in the windows and swirled around their bodies. Godwin knelt over Peter, naked as he, and fucked him, was fucked by him, made them both fucked. Antic windblown scavenger's feathers rustled against the marmorous columns of a ruined temple, the rubble of the altar was set upon by a satellite of purple light, spread over with a giant rippling silk banner advertising devolution, the figureheads cackled, a dome was suspended over the ruins defying gravity and time, and the dome was dropped, shattered, scathed the fabric, rained over the altar in luminescent shards. Then, Godwin did something that made Peter extract himself from her velvet crypt.

I could not ascertain at first what had made him react so violently, I am not privy to the vicissitudes of Godwin's private musculature. Peter pulled back, meaning pushed her back so that she sat up over him as a disdained sphynx, albeit a moving and talking and shit-stirring sphynx.

"No, no, no, no," he said.

Stage direction: *please repeat.* She went in for repetition: she did it again. He whipped his head to and fro. Was she nipping him too affectionately? He tried to withdraw completely from the fray; she would not have it; she tripled down, and I could just make out the offending article: she was plying his ear with something.

"We will not live through tonight . . ."

Reciprocally, he boxed her ear gently then more fervently, sending her face into electric vibration. There came another a bloom of miasma from her throat:

". . . and in this fantastic bloodshed we will deliver ourselves from evil . . . "

Peter took a respectable swipe at Godwin's face.

Folded in the far corner of her bed, Godwin added color, bit by bit and by accident, to the bedspread, that color the same hue as the sternfruit she had left in the bowl close by, and she could not stop herself from laughing. The turns of her laughter folded ribbons of blood into a puddle in her center and into the cave of her belly button and further into tributaries and attendant blood-ponds and pools. Blood leapt over the bottle of anisette she tilted to her mouth. It relieved the pressure somehow on her lineaments. It sputtered and crawed as she laughed.

"Napkin?"

"Hold your nose and swallow."

"My nose is probably broken. Again."

"The features should be a faithful representation of the mind. Your whole face should be broken."

"Napkin? Come on Peter. You must admit…"

"Somehow your idiocy only made sense in combination with intercourse. But in combination with intercourse it was heinous."

"It did bring out the wretched in you. And the beautiful in me. A napkin. A towel. Anything! Ai, it goes freshet."

"Here."

"Thank you."

"Like this."

"Thank you."

"…"

"…"

"…"

(In a nasal voice.) "What do you think Mister Pearlhorn's reaction will be?"

"If you promise to kill the both of you? He will throw you through a window. What's the word?"

"Defenestration. The point is devotion to the point of no return, Peter, and he will devote himself to me, in that moment. He will assent to it all. Not maim me, as you have."

"I feel a wager brimming."

"I bet he gives up the world for a moment of true indulgence. Gives up his entire world of whoredom and uselessness. All his mistresses and paramours, all his curtain girls and vapid snakeswallowing fiends, all his tramp vamps, even his housekeeper, I'll bet she's taking it to the hilt every Tuesday, Peter, I will make him give them up, swear them off forever and ever, make him renounce them and their lives, renounce himself and his own life, and I will return unscathed and satisfied. Perhaps also I will make him renounce literature, art, botany, all that is beautiful and vain, Josfrende, Whitson, his narcissistic wonderland of masturbation, his slimy self-love, his disdain for all worldly ambition. All in a night's work."

"And I bet that that moment of true indulgence is the one in which he defenestrates you. I would have done at least so much, if I were not dependent on your lady parts like crack. And your other parts somewhat, to frame the lady parts."

"It is a fine little lady part, isn't it. Look at . . . it . . . her? . . . it?"

"The finest in the land. Except for Scarlet's, which is less complicated. Hers is the heroin."

"I will have him standing, at the threshold of his madness. I am his madness, you know. And he is a self-loathing husk of a man, without me."

"He will swat you. Or you will swoon in his arms, a coward, demanding nothing."

"Don't insult me Peter. I might just run away with him. To his island, the swooning saint."

"Run away with him, do it. But either he maims you or he doesn't, in the moment. Now. What can we bet on this? Not Scarlet."

"I don't mind taking Scarlet from you again."

"You borrowed her."

"Let us bet a sum of money."

"Money I feel corrupts the purity of the bet. What money?"

"The money you will extort from him, in the meantime."

"Extort from him! You do the extorting yourself. Just marry Pearlhorn and be done. And then kill him, or whatever you need to do."

"Marriage is for the Tickers, or the Hootenwalls. I want to quit whoring my mind to man and become a woman of the gods. Money will do that, you know, ill-gotten or no. It can ennoble."

"If marriage is for the Tickers, then what are you trying to . . . ? You're out of your mind . . . but I guess this is your mind. And since I have nothing better to do . . . "

"I need more napkins."

"You've smeared it wider. Just pinch."

Chapter Sixteen

A metaphor comes to mind, the only metaphor that ever was, that of art to itself. The first theme of art is silence, and how that silence strikes us: the rhythm of the heartbeat. The second theme is symmetry, or what we might call pleasure: the rhyme or dance of elements in harmonious poses. And the third is the movement of the heavenly bodies, the glory of arc, which elevates the individual elements of a composition (water, blood, salt), then drops them to the earth, producing the illusion of completeness, just as the day does. No poem includes all its essential elements, the line is an approximation of itself, which is painted into the mind like a burn, its toes can only point at a footfull of its innumerable coordinates. In the words left unsaid, as the saying goes, there is painted the entire picture. What stems from silence finds its root in silence, there is no other way. So: they are descending the spiral staircase now, Godwin and Peter, they are silent. Godwin is in view, now she disappears from view, now she looks up at him, now she looks away. The spiral turns. He hears her footfalls, they fade from him. The smell of her body, drunken fever and a perfume he will remember for the rest of his life, rises and hovers in the middle air and engulfs him. A gathering of life no more noble than a clack on the earthly dancefloor, he attempts to weave a cord, an imaginary line between the two of them—him, and the packet of chaos and bliss that once was his first love, when love was a thing, and he hers, when they were seven. What are the three themes of Godwin? he asks himself. A drowning, he thinks, the first is a drowning in her body, her body the terrifyingly magnetic vacancy of space. The second is the suicidal fantasy of an impact that peels back the skin of my face, that bursts open all my veins and leaves me exposed to the whipping desert sands and pumice snows of mortality—and then to her only. And the third is a dream, the dream that I can have some pinprick of an effect on her, that I might take ownership of a single one of her multitude of parts, a bead of sweat from her chin. Water, blood, and salt. Or the delirium and terror and worship we owe the gods.

Chapter Seventeen

Mirra Bravo is driving to Lupine, so let us follow her and indulge in a bit of landscaping, ornamental for you, endemic for me, so it goes. Rodkin's springtum and nitent willow poplar ringed with evethorn and sargent's slipper, with fields of blooming tucker's lei interlocking with the fey faces of the olney flower, lead you out of Two Trees, and you flow down the Lindovician moraine left by the Stork glacier, which screed the Forbluffs, the Canfolds, and the foothills of the Rorfillance mountains, crests of which have blown into the ocean, leaving mesas every-where that resemble the tombs of whole cities buried. Armies of beauxtrim spruce climb and conquer these ancient gravehills and are vanquished and replenished by fire in their own shades. Crags pinch and fall away from you. Lights of saltsewn gallow squares and grinch tenements gleam and gloam in the distance. Interminable night sounds wand and swoon in the folds of new-born haze that blanket the air, and the enchanted dolomite spires of Ex and Tarne crowd over you and die behind you leav-ing embers of benevolent whispers. Over a causeway, you seek the heaving pushes of the flintflats, the jeroboam noons and pomadore midnights cultured in the salt air, and they rise and find you and bring you into their fold. You hold your breath another mile: a curve, a lane, a high crifted wall, you are home again, Mirra.

Mirra flies from the car and around the house, miraculous to her in its reflected darkness as a spirit reborn from the underworld. In a flowerbed close by her childhood bedroom window and joyous with fickle rosetarry Mirra relieves herself. She draws from the bottle of tart liquor she has been drawing on the whole way here, this time she draws with special depth. She reaches out from her body to feel the air groused with the pitch of keels and the weight of sails. The ocean air has action in it. The ocean itself mirrors the moon from beyond the vineyard, and everything is revealed by a double light in the double night. Mirra searches, then reaches for Lupo, who, imitating the sailor so far as his taste goes, sleeps in a hammock strung between the spindled columns of the rear terrace, swinging and spinning, swinging and spinning with the earth and seeming an aged child in a womb of canvas, and she slips the watch back on his wrist. Then, latelorn, badgered by time, she falls to the dewdropped stone and sleeps in Lupo's double shade.

Chapter Eighteen

Pearlhorn, wrecked—he has allowed drink into his study, by fault in design (there is a cabinet in the gallery)—fears for his organs and scrolls a number into a phone that coils in crimson lamplight in a windowless alcove, an heptogonal nook bedecked with narn and domed with iverie. Whitson's *Hothouse Hours*, unheeded, rests open on the arm of the chair. Pearlhorn dials, restarts, shrugs and dials again. Ianthe answers, from the other side of the house. They speak in Gallic babble, which I loosely translate.

"I never…"

"You always. Viennes again. The pot is hot."

"Nonsense. I never think. Always? That is past my point of boiling."

"Fine, you never. There is a delay on the brakes of a bus."

"Arrete idiot. I need to get dressed."

"You probably do not."

He hangs up, smiles, peers up through the iverie dome. He sees himself from above, sees himself peer, and it is not a good image, it makes him want to disappear. His face is the ballooned flesh of a cartoon Mongol, and the objects around and upon him, lampshade, cigar box, book, skull, bottle, seem to inhabit an equally barbarian material world, where the language of discreteness is flouted. Into the image comes Ianthe, in a hurry, in her maid's costume, naturally. Her nose and fingers and eyes melt from their backgrounds into the velour of darkness that is Pearlhorn. She muddles his image with hers. Everything is perverted, and perfect.

Chapter Nineteen

Lynch sat all evening in his chair, his eyes rattled by the television set, and his brain punished by the mystery of Mirra's departure and the conundrum of what (or whom) to do first, now that she was gone. Lupo could die in an hour, he could die in a week, that clouded the scope of Lynch's possible paths. He had tried talking to himself, but he didn't have anything to say.

"Kid!"

Peter was home from Godwin's—he never, after the first time, spent the night in her bed. He rose from his volume of Gonagin's *Doric Few* and found the black stairs with the tip of his toe—the upper hall in the Lynch cottage was always darker than night. He descended, muted the television, and regarded his father as he always did, with distaste he could barely mask with disdain.

"I need a beer, kid. And ice."

"There is plenty in the fridge. And freezer."

"How about you get me some. I have trouble getting up just this minute here. I'm hurting."

"You're hurting because you're a drunk."

"A drink or two here and there is not a drunk."

"I think you would rather be a drunk than not, because you are all but utterly useless, unless there is something that needs fucking up."

"I'm not sure that's how you want to talk to your father, kid."

"I'm only telling you what you already know. If you were not drunk, people would take you for a pincushion, because your sober mind doesn't know how to operate."

"What's your point, kid."

" . . . but even pincushions have a place somewhere in the cosmos. Have you ever thought of rising from the beery abyss where you spend your time? Growing arms and legs again? Partaking in substantial pleasures? Have you ever thought of elevating your existence such that you would not fall back into the womb each day? You should think about it."

"Don't talk like a jabberer. Talk normally."

"I speak of possession, of identity with the life that one seeks. I don't think you have experienced this yet."

Peter gave his father the beer and ice, and Lynch opened the beer, forgot what the ice was for, set it down on the coffee table, where it melted over an ashen landscape, and stared straight ahead of him, not so much at the television as at the television dial, which was missing a three. Lynch had scraped off the three following a devastating upset, shown on the marquee sports channel YMC3, of the Kooks by the Birdcats in which the score after eight innings had been eleven to zero in favor of the Kooks. Lynch had performed various acts of vandalism after the loss, including a spectacular and intentional shattering of the door to the back porch with his own airborne body weight; a terroristic raiding of the liquor cabinet and an expensive smashing of a bottle of Lilith Two; and a bat-battering of his own truck. The effacement of the television dial was the most permanent and addling result of the loss, and Lynch had for months considered the possibility of acquiring a white marker. But he could not gather the necessary will to enter an "arts and crafts" store, where he would become so embarrassed and forlorn that he would walk out without buying anything, as he did in all stores. Maybe he should scrape the rest of the numbers off the television dial, to make the whole setup appear more sleek.

"I had hope once, you know, kid, I did. I had ideas of becoming someone else. I had a sense that you could grow, that I would work and somebody would notice, that the future would be different from the past, all that shit. I had all kinds of hope. Maybe I'd stop having to sling a hammer. Maybe I'd get out of this falling down house, or actually buy it. Maybe Mirra, you know. More kids. The whole thing. Not that you're a bad kid, you're not, don't get me wrong, kid, alright? You're a good kid, a great kid. I just think the point is, I'm actually happier now that I gave in, lowered my expectations, I can live without thinking every day about how it could be different. I don't get so bent out of shape every time the Kooks lose. I don't even watch them sometimes, you know? I can appreciate things. Like this beer, which is a beautiful thing. You want one?"

"I'm fine."

"Drink with me, kid. A man should not drink alone. So right, like I said, I don't think you have to shoot the moon every time you play cards. Same in life. But you're still young. You should try and shoot the moon a few times, who knows? And the worst that can happen is you fall slap on your face a few times and learn a lesson. Me, I'm good right here in my chair."

"That's not the motivation I need."

"What?"

"Nothing. I'll try you again in the morning."

Peter went into the kitchen and brought back two beers. He cracked one and slurped at it, staring into the flat face of his father, who was staring at the television set, not so much at the screen as at the dial. Lynch really did need to decide whether to bite the bullet and purchase a white marker, or to scrape the rest of the numbers off.

"Kid, go get me that bottle of Old Strayhand will you, and some more ice please, thank you, pour yourself a finger or two . . . What should we toast to?"

"To mediocrity."

"What?"

"To sloth."

"I'd rather the first one. Sloth is a papal sin, you know."

"And mediocrity is the blessing of the damned."

"I'll take what blessing I can get, kid."

Chapter Twenty

Mirra awoke on the terrace stone in the very wee hours, her whole body in pain, and hobbled inside to her childhood bedroom, the one painted dim blue as it had been when Lupo and Ekaterina had reckoned a boy. A glass eiderfleur stood yet in its hourglass vase symbolizing Mirra, Art, the Continental Divide, and vanity. One wall carried still its burden of books, from Horthian to Canthus and Nivelle to Fond, from Whitson to Whitson; a note had been taped, now was pinned on three sides, to one of the pillars of the bookshelf: *Michael is the son of Aheiu;* and the other three walls gave on the sea, fields, marmorous sky, and a congregation of Weber's papyrus bushes, all in a hurry to go somewhere and hide (the winds blew offshore more than not). The desk, athwart two seagiving windows, was of simple construction, with dull narn inlays. Mirra was unfathomably fragile from sleep and a dream of a banquet of which she was made the guest of honor. It was held not in a banquet hall but in a cavern ringed with ferns and spotted with pools in which vermicular streams of tadpoles darted. She was to give a speech…a speech…Thank you but…I'm sorry, I thought this was, you know, I am looking for someone who isn't here, I am looking for myself, god bless the man who will give me a blanket and a candle, to foray deeper into this cave . . . . She approached the desk and sat down at it, she cleared her eyes and started to see. The note on the bookcase was illegible from where she sat, and she did not care for Canthus or Mannis, so did not see them, rather noticed Whitson and remembered Whitson—my rancid juvenilia, my stubborn obsession with the daughter of a San Marino musician (*Even now I cannot forget her / I wish that we had drowned together*); and she saw how the morning sunlight, made buoyant and holographic by the waves, painted and erased, painted and erased its own landscape on her mind's ceiling from moment to moment. The swells' parade of images plucked at her viola strings. One string grew too taut, and scripped and cried. She sought a pencil and reproduced that flowing, self-extinguishing landscape. With a match she turned the sketch to ash, flushed it down the toilet, and as the sun she began anew.

Aden opened his eyes. The maid was splayed over him, again. Gonfleur was getting sacked again. Judging from the mess and the bottles, Ianthe had gotten sacked again. He was late for school again. He had no lecture to deliver—again—and this day would be another flounder through the depilated forests of his personal inferno. He tried to shake off his doomed fatidic feeling in Ianthe's cold shower under the lavish head that streamed in droplets representing the afterflow of a rain, and he was somewhat successful. He drifted out onto Ianthe's terrace, smoking, looking in at her hairless body in its desultory arrangement, like a splash of pale pink paint expertly launched at a giant canvas to represent the careless energy of youth. To the confused horizon reflected in the doors, he reflected aloud that if he could only be faithful to Ianthe, she would solve all his earthly problems.

Godwin would never admit that over her morning cereal of dried turnfruit, over her eggs done agape, over her xrabra tea, she read the daily papers. Not for knowledge did she read, but for dyspepsia, nausea, rot of the mind, as one with a fully stocked cellar might guzzle raw sherry in the pantry, for no particularly good reason. She took the papers seven or ten at once, so as to suffer fully before having the chance to know what the obverse might bring. This her father Arthur had done, and even her mother in her early days, before she swore off other people's work. This she understood her mother's father Filidel, a minority cramp in the Senate, to have done as well over his Nitwits and Strefons (Filidel had been a lover of sugary cereals), and to have inherited from his father and mother, a pair of Fotic Missionaries to the Jolly Land. The papers were always the same, it could have been the same day's news that she read over and over, but in their effects could be felt some variation in hue, in her mind. For example, Godwin felt a massacre generally as heavenly white, a war as forest green, and a murder as pus yellow. A trial was pinstriped in the colors of the crime; a lie was deep rose pink; an imprisonment was an ironic sky blue. Police chases were horn ivory. Big heists were a thermometer's mercury. But no event partook merely of one puddle on the palate. You had trials over massacres during wartime (alternating

white and green stripes); you had lies about murders after police chases (light baby dung) and so on. Then there was accom-
panying music, depending upon the geographical location of
the tragedy. Today, she heard what she thought was a symphony
in G flat to a background of saffron huts and sailor's warning,
and somebody was trying vainly to blind her with the reflection
of the uric moon in a mirror. There was a picture of a soldier
with his caps blown off, both thinking and fighting, and one
cap was fitted whimsically into the other, as the rest of him lay
some distance away, still fondling his rifle. A fly-studded sha-
man frowned; his rags hung from him as drying laundry. Apes
escaped from the zoos, as well as flamingos and giant turtles,
whose bladders were being harvested for cropwater. A sonata
in F major took you to a market, where beans were boiled in
blood. The face of a child had been rubbed off with an eraser,
then scribbled back on again. Godwin ate her eggs, her cereal,
drank her tea and a half-gallon of water, and hacked everything
back up in the bathroom. She took a quick one of anisette to
cleanse, linxed down five or six pills of different colors and con-
flicting drumbeats, and called for her mother Dorothy, to make
sure she was still alive.

Chapter Twenty-One

Lynch awoke on a difficult seat, his head drooped between his knees, whence wafted a treasonous odor that boggled his senses. Lynch troubled himself to find a stream or pocket of less troublesome air, and failing that, his legs asleep from the squatting such that there was no way to rise, projected a stream of bile and Old Strayhand into the shower curtain. An hour or so later he was downstairs in as ship shape as one could be, considering. Peter sat sideways in Lynch's easy chair, while a review of the skies of tomorrow played on the television set.

"So?"

"Fuck me, what now?"

"Have you thought of a way?"

"A way where?"

"To help yourself. I told you to help yourself, and by now any self-respecting pincushion should have found a way."

"I haven't even had a cigarette, kid."

"You had all night."

"You've always been a strange kid. Give me one…they're there."

"Don't change the subject. Now we have…forty-eight hours to deliver. Roughly. Maybe sixty at the max. And here you stand dithering about cigarettes."

"Deliver what! Hours?!"

"Think about it, Pops. Just think. What does man want more than life itself? What do we *all* want more than life itself?"

"Pops? A cigarette…"

"No not a cigarette."

"I meant…"

"You know, this is an interesting exercise. You cannot think past proximate material needs right now, so I'll go easy on you and extend the exercise. Just take the day and think about it. Think about it, and bring me back an example of something that can transform a man into a higher being."

"A thing cannot transform you, kid."

"This is much more than a thing. Just think about it, take your time."

"Why do you torture me like this, hey? We had a good time last night, I thought. The beer, the whisky, the camaraderie, you can't beat it, and you need to learn to drink kid, or those ponce boys at Ex are going to leave you under the table. Maybe you shouldn't have kept up with me those last few."

"I didn't. You were drinking for both of us."

"Eh well the thirst is a powerful thing, you know? Don't ever get between a man and his thirst."

"Well, you try and get between yourself and your thirst for a moment, and bring me back my magic potion."

Chapter Twenty-Two

Peter, Scarlet, and Godwin had a hidden circle in the compass-less woods behind Marywood School, a circle they inherited by way of a tortured line from certain explorers of the class of 1917, whose gaping initials were carved high in the skin of the paxwood in which the three habitually perched. Paxwood branches radiate from the trunk as the rays do from a childish sun, or as the arrowtails from yesterday's ambush—and each punctual spindle is as strong as a well-placed compliment—thus the paxwood is the sky's ladder and raft. The circle had other advantages. A stream, an early source of the Caritton, continually coated the inner noise chambers from its secret gorge behind a curtain of Pushka's yew, or as they called it in Two Trees, Darling cedar. Glassy-backed boulders shaded and were shaded by each other. Blue olnie noodled around one's feet. You could stay in that circle for three centuries without a thought but pure marvel at the intimacy of the landscape, and then, convinced of your enlightened madness, make your unguinal way up the paxwood from the forest floor to the balcony of the world, and be lofted there until dinnertime. This morning Godwin arrived especially early—the six pills had had little net effect other than making her forget what time it was—and ascended halfway up the tree before the other two arrived. She found a familiar bed of branches and settled in their cradle, where she could lay her head back against the bole and feel the filtered light growing on the world. Awakening god knew how long later, she found Scarlet and Peter loosely twined and asleep next to her. She laid a light sweater over Scarlet's forgiving stomach, firm but soft and even weightless, and made it her own pillow. There passed the moments in white, in deep green and cognac, and Godwin had a dream of a market stall that sold fates. They came in opaque little orbs like zimsan beans, and every time she examined a few, the dirty hand of the hawker, his dirty fingers lightly leaping, admonished her,

"No no, those are mine. Those are mine no no. No no baby girl, those are mine…You must buy, you must buy!"

There were things, dreams before and after, awake and asleep, but I am not your faithful scribe. I am the hand of Lupo's watch, which does not run, does not fly, does not even flee the interminably gone behind it. The hand turns and returns. Just, I wish I could preserve Godwin there, fetal against the womb of her dear friend, and forgetting, forgetting that anything had ever happened or every would. If I could do this just once in my mind—freeze her in harmless bliss, in hot life that does not need to burn outwardly, for the moment—I may set down my pencil, salt the interminable hedgerows that rule my pages, and drive my old Annapurna off a cliff. But baby, baby, that simple fate is not mine. Godwin, the eternal homuncula, stirs.

Chapter Twenty-Three

"Tell me from the beginning. Tell me everything from the beginning."

"*Ai Mirrita*…. I have only so much time. I cannot possibly…"

"Don't look at your watch. It cannot tell you anything. Your blood is still warm."

"Nor did Dooring appear to be dying, when he breathed his last."

"The man was half your age, and he died in a freak accident. He most certainly did appear to be dying, when he careened off that precipice."

"Each death in itself is a freak accident, a slithering of time out of time, an impossible event. I learned of my death in a sterile space that was no better than a nightmare. All the same I have knowledge of it. Why do you not, in the strength of your oblivion as to your end, weave me a quilt of tales to die upon?"

"You should die on a blanket woven in your own style. You do not want to be buried in my rags."

"The stuff of your rags is worthy of the celestial seamstress."

"But you have more yarn, you have lived, I am only beginning."

"What does it matter? You arrived. I am redeemed. I can swim out to the middle of that seascape and take the lifeboat to eternity."

"I had thought you would know enough of history not to use such a word."

"I know nothing of history, nothing of man, only the hue of the light in a certain space of my mind, the sanctum where catalogues to the winds are kept. The subject of those catalogues is eternity."

"There it is. You have begun, Papa."

They had met over Lupo's breakfast, a cheerful meeting, breakfast that went cold with Lupo's watching Mirra prepare hers, a jigger of espresso shot with cayenne pepper and a periluna of croissant nestling a rain of pickled innisfig. He had begun to speak, but she had silenced him. Outside, she had said. He had made stops at his stores of wine, his vines, his coffee trees. He had made marks, not for fear of theft but for fear of thirst. Now they lay on the beach, over the sand of which Lupo had failed to extract a handful just yesterday, saying there was no use, over the place where Mirra had taken her brow beating almost two decades before, a span of time that collapsed in the first moment of speech. Their gazes roved between each other and the few cotton clouds that hovered spellbound over the surf.

"*Yo se que tu amabas carbonara.* I know that you loved that coalminer's dish. But any one of the ingredients alone—grains, cheeses, eggs, cream—you despised."

"This is I, not you."

"No no, it is I. Everything is I. It remains to wait. You will see. So. You despised the ingredients of a thing…the parts. And the same went for polinara. And the same for what they call a sandwich, and what they call a cake, and what they call a sauce, never mind that all three are combinations in themselves. The result was that you could not be fed food as we knew it—agapito from the field, manzatillos, jicaros—you had to be fed some alchemy, so that you could not trace the origin. I can see from your habits that little has changed. I used to make you an agapito and pepper butter sandwich from rice bread, and you declared it good, but only if I ground it into a purée. Your mother used to say that you were a child of Jupiter, that your distemper was more fit to outer space than the planet Earth. She called you other things, too, that I should not mention, such as a shitass, a donkey's daughter, a tramp in noble cloth. You would not drink from your mother's breast if she did not first consume a cuba libre."

"Thank god she did enjoy a drink."

"Yes, but the irony—the overevolution of your tastes—did not stop there. You would not associate with real persons, gatherings of flesh. You favored your imaginary friend, Florido, who was an actor in the theatre. You did not realize that he was already an actor in *your* theatre, and you could have done anything with him that you wanted . . . You had to make him an actor in another, imaginary theatre, and there was a costume room, from which Florido could not depart undisguised. If someone else had the cop suit on, then Florido was a robber. If the man suit was at the cleaners, then Florido was a maid. Once you told me that Florido's human suit had burst a leak, so he had to be a fish for the day. A fisherman caught him and ate him. Florido got to resurrect himself for another round as a man, when his suit was mended. Here I started to understand you, really to know you, as something from me but not of me."

"But you miss something."

"Oh no. I am getting to that. His days off you mean. Yes, his days off. The days when your marionette rested—those were the days when he became you. Not the other way round—not as in Newman Gessa—but the days when there walked a thing on a stage, above you, in that copper and velvet space you had painted up there. When he was you, when Florido became Mirrita, then you saw yourself in your own, your only skin. Here was the dead, or live, end of the pantomime. The skin was captivating, like the ancient desert landscapes of Omeria. And what walked inside the skin was beautiful as the dunes' unseen depths in the night. And you knew it. And your knowledge, not so much vanity as knowledge because what you beheld was real, was terrifying even to you."

Chapter Twenty-Four

"Mirra?"

"..."

Pearlhorn stood outside the bakery, his face to the glass, and
gurgled,

"Mirra?"

"..."

He saw himself in the glass from afar and above, in his own
private cinema—it had been a violent, grueling shooting ses-
sion, the stars were starving and the extras were in mutiny—and
smiled, two- and three-faced, into the camera. His body disinte-
grated and crashed to the pavement. He stood. He saw himself
break the glass wall and dig Mirra out of the cupboard where she
had hidden from him as a figurine, knowing all, eavesdropping
on herself and him all these years—and he pressed his face into
her figurine face as he did against his own reflection. In the living cool of the figurine's false cheek he found the key (a false
key, that vanished as soon as its teeth were hewn) to its understanding of a phantom Pearlhorn, whose imagined reflection
slumped weary, forlorn, and forsaken into a café chair and let its
forehead fall onto the speckled head of a pepper shaker that left

a plaguelike inscription between its eyes. He leaned against the glass. His numbness became that of a captive or castaway who has just earnestly, after years of starvation and solitude, forgotten his own name.

"Mirra."

" . . . "

And his numbness became that of knowledge, that the timing of Mirra's leaving could have been far better. Aden had the ghost of an idea, the last of a head just severed fresh by a guillotine and rolling surprised and shattered into the bloodied basket, that he would not be reunited with her again. Peter, her son, that pretender, that halfwit, would be Aden's only glimpse of the woman he had called for some time his one true addiction—he did not use the common curse-length variant for fear of shooting himself in the face, for love to Pearlhorn was as good as death.

(Aden imagined Peter a halfwit because Peter once, so Aden thought, used the word "croon" so preposterously in an essay that he could not possibly have known its meaning. Aden had not guessed that it was a malformed "crown.")

Aden yawned and forgot himself, why he was there, why he was anywhere, forgot it all and plunged into his Annapurna, which knew him, so Aden thought, better than anyone in the world—it knew him as a preposterous character muttering the name of Mirra and forgetting the utterances and the driving as he muttered and drove. It knew not to say anything and not to do anything of its own volition, or else it would make Aden very nervous. Once it started itself in reverse, and it paid the price: it was given a very painful transmission transfusion. The risings of Aden's own volition made Aden nervous enough. We may tally them:

The staining of his blood with the blood of Mirra, such that the solution was impossible to tell from its parts;

A choosing, at some juncture, long ago, where man's nature met that of nature herself—she once an artist, now a stratum bomb—of the dulling bottle over the sharpened pencil, poetry over prose;

That thing with his student;

A bad quarrel, this morning, with Ianthe, again, because no matter how many times he showered her with affection, she was taking vacation just when he needed her most;

The perpetual hanging of the jury on his intellect, hung as the jury was by his sloth and his too-thorough vision a sloth and a sharpness that would not abate; and

The spending of half a million this year, on wine mostly, and things he couldn't identify, such as whores whose names he could not recall, not professionals of course, more like amateur whores, situational whores, and it was only June.

"Half a million."

When he put everything merely this way, it was not so horrible.

Chapter Twenty-Five

"And you're fine with that?"

"I've never been fine with anything. And no one has ever given a hoot."

"But your thoughts, Peter. Your thoughts."

"I think that my thoughts are subordinated to a higher power, for which my thoughts are slaves and my actions are the farcical viceroys. That higher power is Godwin."

"Then I will say it. If she does this, if she gets too close to Pearlhorn, she will never be the same, Peter. He will fuck her up. He has done it already, without doing anything."

"But she is never the same, night to night, morning to morning. She is the wave that scrapes the shore in a million different ways."

"She has an orbit that one can describe. She has—a center about which she turns, and that center is . . . "

"A fragrant body that we cannot resist."

"No! It is you and me, Peter. She is a vagrant in spirit but somehow wanders back to us. After this, after she wanders away, she will be gone. Godwin gone, and we godless."

"She should escape though, Scarlet. That is the large part of why we burn for her, because she will, as a rule, get away."

"And what about me, why do you . . . burn for me?"

"Because you are a glorious, beautiful, firebreathing fiend."

" . . . "

They were so young. A jungle cream tirenta inspected Scarlet's face. She tried to pick at its wing, missed, tried again, and caught the lockamure the tirenta was hunting. Peter and she lay back over a fine find of crift, which shacked and befriended their necks and wept in their ears. Scarlet felt her stomach where Godwin had been. Godwin was no longer there. She had risen.

"And you will never leave."

Now comes Pearlhorn down the Marywood hall. His hands flow weary and chaotic past his sides and flounder his jacket astray, picking up, from across a loose cluster of teasing and rollicking and generally bored nameless students, the Romanesque gaze of Godwin. He touches a palm to the arctic of his hypostatic skull, whose scorched sand he doubts will ever see rain again. Dry lightning pain whips miscellaneous shade over its latitudes. Pearlhorn she. Godwin he. Godwin he tries to forget for a moment. Godwin tucks her blouse deeper into her skirt. She finds his face, and her body bleeds heat and trying. Her body hisses, flashes, flames, dissipates, cracks. My god my god, she whispers. My god my god. And the pressure is too great, it pushes them slightly apart as they pass one another. They pass: he does not look, she does, even searches for a handhold on his back, lest she need to cling to him as he drifts away. Alone again, frightfully alone, she retreats to the bathroom. She searches out the mirror. Her face: What was once a porphyry whole has become a massacre of want. Her frown and neck are stitched with color. Too much, too much. She finds a stall, folds once, and asports handfuls of her olnic hair.

"I am not enough. Not not not not not enough."

Handfuls of her hair, to keep them from the bits and rancor that flee her open mouth. Cold pudding of yesterday. A stromboli shell. A cote of ginger cookies. Canned mussels. Icthic acid. A burger. Some anise. Notice, no racketfruit bits, no eggs. Breakfast was gone, she was down to last night's bonanza. The pressure of the disgorgement nearly tore her eyes from their seer. When she finished, she did all that could be done: she sat half naked athwart the toilet and slept against the wall of her cage.

Chapter Twenty-Six

That afternoon at the Muc Salach Pub in our city of Tarn, cool-headed Lynch entertained his comrades, and they sat around him in a cluster of dull bald or hatted heads, listening for his next word. The architecture of the bar recalled that described by Rial in his *Twenty-Four Years of Scotch and Ice,* though Lynch's bar was filthier and warmer. At one time or another, Lynch had carried on no-nonsense affairs with all the regular women, none of whom were particularly attractive. The irregulars sometimes impressed. This evening, Doctor Theresa Gold was on display. No one had ever seen her before.

"I thought of getting that girl, that woman, she's more of a woman, no? For my son. No not that one. *That* one. Yes. The nurse, must be a nurse, or a dental assistant. For my son. My son has this idea that a man can retry, retool . . . ? He said I need to retrofit myself. And bring him home a new piece of ass, as evidence of the transformation."

"That's some hubris!"

("Hubris" was one of Lynch's comrades' only "words." The only other words they used were unprintable.)

"I think you should . . . "

Here his comrade suggested that Lynch feast on the rear part of the woman.

"She's too beautiful to do that to."

"She's a doctor. She must know her anatomy. Jesus. I'd hang myself just to . . . ."

Here the comrade evoked a scene wherein the woman made water in which the comrade, tangled in a noose, somehow swam.

"How do you know she's a doctor?"

"Because she's dressed in that suit. What do you call it? I would let her shit on my chest."

"Scrubs. She is probably hairy as a donkey under there."

"She's a mental patient or something."

"An unusual bitch."

"That asshole over there's already talking to her. Look at that . . . "

"Get in there, Lynch."

Lynch approaches. The woman's interlocutor gives him no heed, the woman even less, if such be possible. He notices that the two are playing yard games with each other's genitals. He bucks up to the bar, he sways his behind into the woman just a touch, and slaps his pint glass down on her napkin.

"What?"

"What what?

"Who?"

"I don't know."

"Hey."

"Hey yourself."

"We're still sitting here, if you don't mind."

"We? I doubt it."

"Oh. I think I want him. He is beautiful. You, go away. Need to wash my hand."

Here came a round of applause from Lynch's comrades. But they could not see what he could see, that the girl was so drunk that her (admittedly beautiful) face was trembling with toxicity.

"What is your name oh beautiful one?"

"Don't call me beautiful. Peter. What is yours?"

"You can call me Theresa."

"What is the name your mother named you?"

"I prefer to forget her, and her entire race. She was Wiggar, and screamed a gypsy curse when she leapt from the roof of the Rollins Tone Motel into a dry pool. I like your moustache. It makes you look like Arbin Shooter."

"Who the hell is that?"

"Do not mind me. I will call you Arbin. Arbie for short."

"Where do you come from, kid?"

"Kid. That is offensive. I am well past the age of consent. Too old to be sorry. I come from work. That is all you now, or ever, need to know."

"Most of what happens after this is going to be offensive."

"Don't push it . . . Pietro? Pietro. I just emp. I just emptied the chamber pots of human minds all day. That was all the dirt I cared to handle, Arbusto. Arbusto!"

"Alright, then get your filthy chamber pot carrying hand out of my pants then."

"You're married, likely to a worthy woman. What do you want other than this unworthy nonsense? Why do you even speak to me, you despicable man."

"It's not what I want. Not that I don't . . . . It's just, you are what someone else seems to need. If I read him right. Although if I read him right here, it will be the first time I do. My son."

"Incestuous liaisons. I am not well learned in this nonsense, and do not wish to be."

"No, this kind of nonsense you do have lessons in, Theresa."

"Are you going to bring me home and fuck me? I'm tired. I do not mean to be vulgar. I am not this way, in the daylight. Kiss me, by the way."

Theresa Gold wavers, and in her orbit she brushes against Lynch's face. Her eyes do not leave his except to waver too, with the rest of her. Her free hand dithers in the hairy space between his shirt buttons. Her unfree hand waylays the neck of the (slightly) crooked prehistoric terrapin in the space between his legs. Their orientation is as a silent movie fitted to arbitrary music and caption. Tenderness and trouble. A waking to a nocturne. Or do you like this kind of thing? Lynch himself is in his best form; he feels fit to overflow. The good doctor's touch is precise.

"I need to piss."

"So do I, well said Arnoldo. Meet me here, please please. Do not stray from me, I will have my revenge."

He leads her to the ladies' room and gives her a light push through the door, with some last moment guidance to her slipstream. He bursts into the men's room and finds the trough and celebrates with a whistle over himself. Will it heed him? It will. Why do I never shave my moustache? This would be the right occasion. But the kid. But the kid. Fuck the kid, fuck the kid, he can wait his turn. Lynch pisses, finishes, and waits at the bar for a sign of Theresa. None issuing, he smokes outside, checks the environs, and beats back to the bar for another drink. Still no sign of her, he smokes outside again.

A sound like a bitten mammal arises in the distance. The mammal strides, howls, weeps, roils, drones. An ambulance wails into the gravel lot. Its lights flash apocalyptically against the not-yet-night. A team of medics extract from the Muc Salach what could be Theresa, with a mangle of tubes leading to her from stray angles. It must be her, for there was no one in that bar half as fucked up as Theresa Gold. Lynch waves to her, and with the other hand he shrugs.

"Drunkenness," he says.

Now the "real" Theresa Gold runs from the bar with a thousand dry eyes and the scent of pollen-dusted rills and half-shaded riverbanks following her. She has freshened up.

Chapter Twenty-Seven

Just as Theresa Gold is more than she seems, just as you are more than you seem, Aden Pearlhorn is more than he seems. Far more, even. And less. He is nothing and everything. He is potentially ruinous and utterly and gloriously useless. He is a very rich man and a very poor man. He hates adjectives, he would pole me just now with his cane. So let us simply listen.

Renunciation is the last thing left to King Fear, but he cannot accomplish it. This is what kills him, of course. This is what kills him.

Pearlhorn reclined in his office. The sun pushed the lowest and nameless tropic, the Tropic of Tantrum, having sailed through the day again heartless and glorious as a puncture wound in the sky. Aden wondered what he had missed today. Not missed in terms of the works of Josfrende, the author of *Ballyhoo About Something*, whom he knew as well as the translucent back of any wine label gazed through the glass. He wondered not what he had missed as an intellectual, but rather what he had missed in terms of God…Godwin. She had entered the classroom a full hour late, meaning when the space had emptied of students, and had stared at him in the doorway for a full hour more before speaking, and then barely a word ("I . . . "). Something about her had looked infected. Her hair not blonde but jaundice. Her eyes not narnic but tumulous. The body against the doorpost in, so it had seemed, incapacity. Tell me she was incapacitated with . . . he proffered the word but it did not stick to his senses. How many days has it been since she looked at me like that the first time? How many days have I worshipped her in the morning to renounce her in the afternoon, to kill myself for her in the evening? How many days has she been sick like this, and I flatter myself that she is sick for me? But then why does she stand this way in the doorway? Then why does she stand this way in the doorway? And why, and why . . . .

Godwin stood in the doorway, about to fall, and Pearlhorn did not have the presence of mind, read the courage, to loose the strings of her silence. He needed a prompter to feed him his lines, though he knew them. You could say, he needed me to tell him he had an hour yet to live. It is afternoon now, time for renunciation, but what tools of renunciation do I have, thought Pearlhorn, besides the blunt ones I used last, which merely numb and do not kill. And even if I could kill—to kill a sadness is to widen its mouth. Say my goodbyes. I should let the two of them destroy each other. I want to be alone, with the maid. Ianthe. But the maid is gone.

Afraid of going home, afraid to move, afraid of what was yet undone, very little and terminal, or very much and terminal still, Aden slid off his chair and lay down on his carpet. When his spine found gravity and sank to the floor, he thought to himself that there was no greater ecstasy than the sense of the earth gripping one.

Chapter Twenty-Eight

"You were already in there, and alone with him!"

"I know, Peter."

"You didn't arrange anything?"

"No, Peter."

"Hum."

"Don't spurn me. I do not spurn you."

"No, Katherine. Simply, it's no business of mine."

"That's even worse. Do not abandon me."

"Do not abandon your cause, your religion. Sin."

"Oh Peter. You know, my part is quite a bit more difficult. I am feeling like the wrong kind of creature. A pickworm, a fungo, a fopfish. You, you are still human. Apollo is human. Whoever I worship is not."

"I just mean, the timing. We need to be in temporis."

"Don't speak of it. Why so itchy, Peter? You are not new to this, this dance we do."

"I am somewhat new to things that don't involve my . . . mere beneficence. Like the time with Art." (Art Pillar was a painter twice Godwin's age who had for long intervals tolerated Godwin's mother.) "Or the time with the rocket scientist." (An experiment gone exactly as planned.) "Or the time you made me…*ech*." (An experiment that had not gone as planned.)

"Ha! I didn't *force* you do it."

"The whole point being so you could say this."

"I don't know. I think it was a worthy thing."

"The point is never that a thing is worthy. The point is that it is unspeakable. I did the unspeakable. Now you do the unspeakable and get it over with."

"But I am tired. So tired!"

Peter and Katherine were up on a low limb of the paxwood, just above the crown of Scarlet, who was picking at cheeks and eyelashes of olney at the tree's base. Scarlet hooted up at them as if they were far above, up where the light still hovered waxlike and in secret places florid,

"If I were you, I would be tired of razor's edge near-profligacy, when the thing itself is not even that profligate."

"But I feel, Scarlet. I feel something in my hands and throat, and in the tingling surface of my face, as if I am about to be executed. The danger of pausing while walking a wire. Suddenly the entire sparkling world below looks like death. Why can I not open up some distance between flying and dying? I want a moment, I want a day, one day, one single day, without the abject debasement of my spirit."

Peter looked Godwin in her eyes, one then the other, and back to the one. Real quick back and forth blue to blue—no

difference, but he wasn't looking for Janus in her—he was looking for the third eye, and the fourth, the fifth. He was looking
for eyes to pullulate from her ears, and a sky-eye to shine on
her head, looking for something other than the disquiet he saw
there, in the two blues.

Chapter Twenty-Nine

"Do you see the problem with this?"

"You are telling the story of my life. Of course I see a problem with it. My life is one big round polished problem."

"But the central thing. The real thing at the center. The balliol, so to say."

"Problems don't have balliols. They have dark cores, nothingness in their hearts. That is the problem with problems."

"You are so young, Mirra. I am surprised yet still it is true. When you get old, you will find a temple to seat your mind up on. In your nook there you will rock as a baby."

"What a terrible thought. Life without madness. Is that where you are now? Kill yourself before time runs out. I brought a gun."

"What good is a gun? The baby rocks not without madness. Death stares me in the eyes even on my narnic altar to the sun, I do not say I live sanely, I would not know what that meant. Who or what is my litmus?"

"What does it look like?"

"The altar. It is before you. Here, look at it."

"Not that. The thing staring at you. The face of death."

"It looks like . . . it has no look. The face of death has no look."

"Don't cop out, Papa. Say it for yourself."

"Questions. Why is the ocean not enough? Why are the fields—not enough? Why do I dream of another turnfruit while I eat the one. The answers are all the same. Why is the sky, why the clouds, why the sun himself not enough? Oh Mirra. You know it for certain. They are not enough, because the work of the gods bears no human imprint, and we do not recognize what we have not touched. Touched, it is a pugilists' term, at its heart. You will recall its usage in my monograph."

"It means to paint with blood."

"Do not take shelter in metaphor, Mirrita. It does not become you."

"It means to destroy."

"Not so much completely to destroy, but piecemeal, as a razor scrapes a bit of oil away from a canvas. I have this sense that every cup must overflow. That every cup must overrun with what be in it. I do not see you dialectically. I see you in a single sweep that became a storm, that became a landscape, that searched out a wanderer to touch, and the nearest one was itself. What now can be done?"

"To begin with, you can tell me what the face looks like, so that I might evade its gaze for so long as I may. And so that I can recognize it when it approaches me. I do not want much Papa. I want peace."

"My heart is cracking in my throat. Bless you, and wake me if the tide rises."

He drifted off, and Mirra away. Droves of tarncreepers limericked and boasted in the sand. She touched her feet to the water. Her feet remained, amid sunspark and birdprint and wavelip and ashy sud, and so she too remained, for a time. If thoughts could speak with turns and stops as a page speaks, though we know they cannot: She knew . . . I know I have felt this way for a long time, and I feel its color and radiance. This way, this way and having color, having direction. No question nor attempt at relating one thought to another by blood. Nor one experience to another. Nor experience to thought—my memory as partitioned as my dreams. My dreams no less voluntary than my waking. I see a line out there, a slight tume in the spine of the earth, that receding line where the visible and the hidden meet, and which by its essence is unattainable. To cross that line, to reach my hand out and caress that line in fact (not simply to caress it in concept, as my impressionist's hand will do), would be easier than to trace myself back to an origin in spirit. Still I feel that I have been in that place, and that I am falling back there—into ground or into space, I cannot tell—and falling or someway else I cannot tell—but falling back or sailing back without harm and without regret, without burden even—falling back over a space I have traveled before.

Mirra drifted further. She kept to the tide line, and the creepers flooded this way and that. Each step was followed by a question—whether she was in sea or on land, and what state, life or death, that meant was waiting for her in the second act— the second act that would not come. These are the musings of a child. What is a child then?

Chapter Thirty

"The most reliable thing in the world is perfect silence. It will turn all the lights out in my skull, the artist that illumines the operas and operatories and olivia groves of my dreams will put down her brush; and my mind, what remains of it, will float away and burst over a foreign city, or over the sea. What prevents me from breaking apart at any one moment? So far, and far as I can see, I am attracted to what is forbidden, forbidden by what authority I really don't care. Ianthe is always that necessary bit off-limits. Godwin is untouchable by sole virtue of the fact that she is Godwin. And now, both Mirra and not-Mirra are forbidden. A pleasant enough duality—Mirra is as distant to me as the thought of leaving her—the same duality I express toward myself. Whitson's, *Let us exchange eyes before / We exchange glances, so you will / See no less of yourself than when / You dreamt me up—*"

Aden loitered behind Mirra's bakery, in the dark. The yard was walled and treed and bakeried on its sides, and the resultant amphitheater, attended by funereal odenrome, its leaves etched feathers itching and antlering the air, was overgrown with trintalia; its floor was fine dust over burgundy-veined numis. Here he had enjoyed, in better days, his pregnant solitude while waiting for Mirra or not waiting, smoking, fearing, watching her through the open door to the kitchen, his darkness to her light. Then his deliverance would come. Her outline, first confused by the apron fluttering off and away, would quiesce. The undulate pain of surfeit would spread over the inner surface of his skin, his guts. He saw her in the doorway, saying,

"All day I steam, I wheeze, I rise, I ripen. All night I harden, I crust, I stale, I rot. For you. What do you do? You hide, you hide. You smoke, you shit, you sleep on your couch. You whimper on the breast of Ianthe. Poets. A fine, delicate, precious species of sloth. And I your whore. I."

And then,

"You are my dream Aden. My one dream. I do not even care who you are in any verifiable sense. My vision of you, reinforced here and there by your actions, your words, has seduced me entirely. You can hang me from this coat hook, and my ghost will return to stand here and watch you waste this moment in dim thought of a line that escaped you. There is something in your manner, your style, an affected sort of suffering that dulls what would otherwise be a Napoleonic air of triumph, levels you off at *addict*. The alcoholic, the drug addict, sure, but more importantly the addict of the night, strung out from the shades of suffering it imposes on you but always dying for more."

Chapter Thirty-One

Lupo awoke to Mirra moonlit against the backdrop of moonlit ripples and fury. She had brought him a bottle of wine (and a bottle for herself) on a platter with an odd number of round peppered chocolates and a half-eaten pear caked with honey and a tussle of cold terridome, a combination of oily meats. Her body was wrapped in a blanket tiered with osirises and cleopatras, warriors and elephants, bacchi and ariadnae. Her hair was salted into thick black rays parading apart. She had been swimming.

"*Tu empezaste de pensar…*Then you began to think. I remember you began to think, because you would go into your bedroom looking slick as a matador, and you would emerge from your bedroom looking old as the matador's mother."

"And he lying gored."

"When you were ten or twelve your eyes appeared as old as those of the legendary wooly haggis. There was the impression that you had been drugged. Your friend yourself, the Sunday creature, she challenged you to a duel, a battle to the death, and you did all you could to beat her in a fair fight, but you cannot beat yourself in any sort of fight. Phantoms will outlive the universe, for the simple reason that their absence is impossible to prove."

"As well is their presence."

"I do not need to prove a presence. To say a thing is to bring it into being. Just, there is not an easy and good way to unsay a thing. In your case the thing you have wanted to unsay is yourself—your self that you invented, that became you, and in the end you swallowed her, but yet she persists. Persists in the very pond of air from which she was plucked. That has been your problem. Now if you'll excuse me."

"To what?"

"No, just let me think."

"This wine is good. Good good this wine.

"Stop, you're in my moonlight, and give me wine, please, death is near."

"You laugh now, finally."

"And that image of the moon behind you is straight from the shelf of my finest memories."

"It is too bad my mind does not shelve. Nor have furniture. Waterlogged. Reefs. Caves. Little clicks. You split me in two— you split a sea in two—an image and its reflection, but neither of my essence, not that I can feel. The image can devour the reflection—the phantom can devour the phantom. Yet I remain. I still stand here. And you cannot explain to me truly how I stand, in what state, in what attitude and spirit and itinerary. You cannot tell me. I cannot even tell you. No measurements in the drift. There is no bell that rings when you hit the mark with your words. And then assuming there is one, and it does ring: after the bell, then what?"

"Oh but the bell of harmony will ring, and does. And then, if it does not, why the gift of speech? If not to give the most reliable clues possible of its bearer's state, attitude, spirit."

"There is no gift that lets me compare my speech with the silence that fills me, to see if the two make a good facing translation of each other. On one side a world of echoes, creaks, clicks again, footsteps, rotations orbiting rotations into infinity, on the other a symbol, or a sentence. A death sentence."

"Ah but Mirra! You have just said it. Footsteps. It is from the soles of our feet that first arise the tones and rhythms of speech. Song. Poetry."

"You speak of form. I speak of substance."

"But there now *you* are splitting a sea in two."

He spoke from his body, a subterranean flow just air-struck and about to cool out of phase into eternity. His eyes no longer swam but lodged in their atlases as monuments of themselves.

"I cannot tell you who you are, that is true. That is impossible. What we are we can never see. We can never levitate ourselves out of ourselves and look the thing over while at the same time knowing what we know and remembering what we remember. People speak of mirrors. Artists speak of mirrors. But mirrors are nothing but carbon copies of the same low forms that bind us to ourselves in the first place—the low form being that child's dull sense of symmetry—so long as we make them, they cannot extend beyond symptoms of our weakness, our blindness. And if I cannot tell you who I am, I who carry and ride myself everywhere, I who inhabit my every space, then I cannot tell you who you are, that is true. But still I can speak! And what I say is more than a mirror. It is all crooked and if you turned it about it would look like the scratchings of a branch against a window in a storm, or the playing of the wind on the glassy shallows. But what is more true than those claw marks, those streams of the skies' consciousness?"

Mirra rose on her toes. On her inside surface beatitudes of a lighter color rose and strife of a darker one fell. So too did hunger rise, not the bodily hunger, one she could not place a price upon. Forms of dairy, owl spotted meats, water, drink, substance, pleasure would not do. Divine hunger: no thing would do.

Chapter Thirty-Two

Peter arrived home to find Theresa Gold lounging in his bathtub. Her exposed parts, especially her somewhat deflated breasts, glistened unctuously. Her face was slightly out of focus with intoxication, and when she spoke it seemed that her muscular signals were being scrambled by a clownish demon working the buttons in the engine room of her skull.

"Oh. Hello there."

"Hello yourself. This is my . . . well not any more."

"Peter did not say to you?"

"Say what to me?"

"Say something. Doctor Theresa Gold."

"Peter Lynch. Doctor. Yes, well, no, he didn't say anything. He's passed out in his chair. What would he have said? Or maybe don't tell me."

"That I am a gift to you. Or demonstration of something . . . a demonstration of something."

"Idiot."

"What?"

"Nothing."

Theresa Gold turned the tap of the tub with her uncannily elegant toe, in such a way that Peter was supposed to notice. Peter washed his hands in the sink, not what he had come for, but it gave him the chance to raise his gaze into the mirror and see the girl from another angle. She was looking straight back at his reflection. Her eyes, in their fogged and lazy-lidded dissonance of focus, and her pruned hand that pulled at the damp ends of her matted hair, were trying to say in not so many words what her mouth soon produced, with no more ceremony than if she had been ordering Peter off a menu of assorted experiences.

"I would not mind being fucked by you."

"Excuse me for a minute."

He went down the hall and out onto the osprey perch that made up the landing, and blinked hard to redact the verdure from his vision. The darkness at the top of the stair was electric darkness so thick that it pooled in the air. He felt through obscure space and into a two-door choke that led to the master bathroom. Here with some urgency he sat on the toilet in the light of a nightlight and, after a moment in mental and physical darkness, entertained his thoughts. His first impression of Theresa Gold was not so glowing as Lynch's had been, yet as his father's exemplar of what can ennoble a man, she was not awful. She was a bit old, but putting that aside for a moment, the girl's foot was worthwhile as a foot. Toes in proper evolution. No terribly protruding veins to speak of. Some blue ones, for sure, but he had forgiven worse. Shins looked fairly smooth, pubis unshaven though not so badly kept (albeit with everything drowned and refracted there remained a chance of ill surprise).

Stomach soft, breasts still somewhat upturned, nipples pale and small—the little silver dollar nipples were her most redeeming feature. Her face was just barely aboriginal, some Hapland back in one of her grandmothers, a Fonita horizon in the eyes, Rouladine in the nose, and Flacon in the cheeks, all in all more than a touch of a brush less than perfect in its potpourric composition. And again, she was quite a bit older than he was. He thought he had espied a wrinkle behind her ear. The quality of her behind was dubious.

"I'm all pruny,"

she said from the other room, and it sounded that she was getting nearer. I should expect some kind of birthmark, he thought. A pimple in an unspoken place, which you see at the last moment before it is too late. A bald spot, a gingerbread flaking of the scalp which you catch in the grabbing when it is far too late.

"Ai! Oh . . . oh . . . oh . . . "

Came from the stairs, and then there was a scuffle with the banister, and a pregnant airborne silence that lasted longer than it did (such moments before impact are so bitterly cavernous). A heady and heavy and distant doom of noise followed, giving way to an even heavier and headier silence, in which Peter now dwelt. He finished his shit with absurd ceremony. He was different, he was not different, he could not decide. Different in that he no longer considered Theresa a prospect, no longer seemed to have the right. And different in that a steam borne pressure forced towards the cap of his skull, with the only exit the eyes and mouth and nose, like a factory whistle. His body began to tingle with idiocy, with pain at the pain of the silence. The pressure intensified when he blinked again at the top of the stairs, descended to the kitchen floor, and saw, thanks to the distant alien strobe of the television, black spots, the color of renatta and kole, volewood, and floods, and growing around Theresa's postimpressionist head.

Chapter Thirty-Three

"Where are you Scarlet?"

"Nowhere."

"Don't say nowhere. I'm struggling. Come back to me."

"I am not leaving. You are weak. I am strong. Why are you not strong?"

"Ex ex. Annie Set. Anais Ette. Draw the world in two colors and you will always be one or the other. To what end, Scarlet? I could suck the blood of a cigarette. If only it had blood. I could suck the blood of a windchime, if only it had blood. So many living things are not alive. Am I less than an organ pipe? Am I the vapid soul of the organist?"

Godwin had her eye on a fat urn in the corner of the sitting room, she had tried to crawl towards it, but had been thrown aside by a mysterious gravity. Etched into the urn's face were two tonsured equestrians, and what looked to Godwin like a curly haired fish or cloud spirit giving advice to a bitter queen. The bitter queen would not tilt her scepter towards the spirit, no matter how importune the carp or god seemed. Tilting the scepter meant what exactly?

"You aren't listening to me."

"You aren't saying anything."

"I am saying everything Scarlet. You do not hear me. I am saying it. Are you listening?"

"I am not listening."

"Oh god damn it, I forgot it all!"

"Be patient with yourself, Katherine."

"There is never anything you can do, Scarlet, and there is nothing anyone else can do. There is only this, Scarlet, only this. And I've forgotten it. It was just here, in my mouth. It was just here…Foal something…Go something. No!"

"Make babies. Get fucking wasted. What else has there ever been?"

Scarlet stretched herself over the couch. She reached over her head and slagged a beaker of liqueur into her mouth, swallowed. A dimple quivered in her smile. The syrup locked her in drift. The inhuman effort of raising herself onto the couch had been well worth it. She began the game of chance—last chance—the game of last chance, where the participant, unsure of whether or not she will awaken, chooses one image to take to Hell with her. In case it was unclear, the two had bushwhacked their way into a thicket of drunk. Scarlet chanced—she last-chanced to want to take with her the feeling of reaching for Godwin but finding her not there, so she reached for her—waved her hand at the pocket of breathing in the darkness, the cast of light on the girl, the many shades of palms and fingers that kelped at the ceiling, the Lotharingian patterns on the carpet, the empty vase, and the voice.

But Godwin was not done. There comes a power from realizing that one is suddenly alone. She boiled and lifted. She turned Scarlet on her side and folded her arm, which had been hanging out over space in a harpist's flourish, and wandered. She gurgled up the several staircases, and washed into the vitrine studio where Dorothy's canvases were born. In this womb they breathed, miraculously, though incomplete, out in the airy open, or behind cotton sheets. Godwin could make out a knight, a dream heath, a castle turned folly by fire; a rainy, pregnant Calliope, a sky full of electric faces and whales; a marble janissary domed with Gordon's ivy, guarding a garden of spired rumback and spreading lewe and black uxan surrounding a circular pond. These were the uncovered. The covered Godwin never unveiled, out of respect for Dorothy and the knowledge that she would find many blank or barely commenced commissions Dorothy had slept on for months or years.

"Who there?"

Dorothy herself slept behind a painted screen, on a sofa made for every possible occasion of repose. Her skin glowed in piano black streams of shade striped with piano ivory streams of moonlight. Her breasts lay astonished and awake, her stomach hungry, her leggy lowers tied in a monk's knot. Her eyes were her daughter's, such a sea bottom of turquoise sand you would guess it painted in.

"Who there?"

Dorothy's theory on Art ran something like this: It made her want to kill herself, but the slow feeling of suicide was too good.

"You here. You know you are here in error. Wander away little one. This is where I perpetuate, alone."

"How many people have you loved mother?"

"How many loved? Probably all that ever lived. Each one in his soot and cry. His jet, his drool. His tripe and tool. But who cares? Where's my wine? I'm thirsty."

"Here."

"Dryish. A bit more in this glass. Good. How about you?"

"Don't change the subject."

"I deeply apologize."

"But then, how do you dwell eternally in silence? Your solitude."

"It is not so to me. When you came into the room, in your violent way, I had just met the savior in Purgatory. He ripped out my eyes and I saw colors and shapes the universe cannot produce. And if you let me back to my, what you call, silence, I will rejoin him and see my soul split once and for all."

"You are lost in dreams like an exiled monarch."

"You are a wretched girl. You miss my gaze entirely. Entirely miss my gaze. I mean to say we are never without suffering for some other being's sake. Even the imagined savior must carry his heart in his purse. Have a drink."

"I already had drinks. Many drinks. And your wine is dry."

"Well then, go yourself to the savior with what power you have."

"Aren't you cold? Your skin is all fleshy."

"I prefer to bathe in air, as the gouty saints do in Paradise."

Dorothy spread out over the couch and heaved a deep sigh. Godwin climbed up next to her, but she could not sleep, her heart raged against her skull as if any moment it would blow out her ears. Not realizing by what impulse she moved through the house, and deriving lessening pleasure from the divorce of mind from body, she sought her bathroom: she needed to void herself. She bent over the bathtub. Anisette cascaded against the backs of her teeth and sprayed sunburst in all directions over the porcelain. Again. And again, until she heaved drily and moaned from her depths where it seemed a monastery of monks were chanting their orisons. She washed down the fluids with cold water from the shower and stripped down and stood in the stream for an indeterminate period of time. Things began to improve. Freezing and shivering but rudimentarily content she climbed into her own bed and smiled at the ceiling and thought, I believe I have arrived at that one thing I can do. I don't know if I have the word for it, it could be reclamation, redemption, call it what you want, it has the flavor of the baptism I just underwent, it has the color of a massacre, as it happens, the heavenly white color of a massacre.

Chapter Thirty-Four

"Just know, just know. Just know I. Just know I cannot. Just know I cannot what?"

Mirra tried to practice her speech. The phone rang on the other end like sardonic laughter, or the clatter of snowy track-breaks under the inertial wheels of her confusion. She had already dialed Pearlhorn again, she dialed again again, the swallow of whiskey went down hot with a sprig of alimon to chase, and her teeth bickered with the drib of a piney cigarette whose smoke wilted in the library's vault. The shrill softness of a tera-pete's wings played in her ear, a softness that she captured and fashioned into an inkwell for a fingerprint of her blood on the ronewood table.

"Aye roo the daye ye ferst sawe ma. Aye roo the daies I left in ye."

She felt besieged by toxicity, and she became more mute with each entry of Pearlhorn's number, which she may well have botched, forgetting—forgetting why she came here, why she would ever come here, and, more immediately, why she was on the telephone. She dialed again again again again. The telephone wearied as the bottle waxed more robust and huge over her. There was so much whiskey left in the bottle that it could, she thought, holding it there up to the lamp, tailor her with a new mind. Tailor me, she thought, with a mind that does not rue constantly from both sides. I cannot imagine a state of the world that I would not kill. He—I want to kill him dead before he dies. There is the gun. But the moment he dies I want to breathe life back into him, slap him awake like a baby, slap him awake and hold him in his flimsy skin and kill him again. Kill death and life both. So washed in blood I would be, I would finally be clean. Nothing more to do.

"Drink Mirra. Drink."

She whispered her stage directions to herself. There was nothing left for Mirra to do but kill Mirra and revive her like a ghost. A ghost. I want to be a ghost. A ghost's ghost. A ghost cannot lose her mind if she is all mind and nothing more. Do that in italics, yes. All mind and nothing more. What do I do, think sideways? *All mind and nothing more.*

"Drink drink."

The phone was still ringing. She widened her gaze and rediscovered her surroundings. In the carpet, a hanging garden of pomegranates decorated a jubilant dance of house and barn animals around a pyre of human slaughter, and the colors setting off the spines of the books that papered the room's walls recalled the numb, astonished faces of so many spectators at that sacrifice. A banker's desk with the smug blank face of a banker presided over the sacrifice. As all desks of such men as

Lupo seem—men who finish things—the desk was too clean for the work that had been done there. Lupo's publications burdened three sets of shelves in the far end of the room—the famous study of familial strife, posthumous impeachments of presidents and kings, monographs on the third and seventh Kilpatrick wars—formerly the most understudied, now the subject of a line of dramas by Teffinger—a farcical memoir on rural solitude in the manner of Lynnoc, an investigation of the linguistic harmonies of the Ullon tribes of Farr—and hundreds of articles using words like "evinces" and "perpetrates" and "discredits" and "fatidic". But the desk was clean; it held not even a paperweight for the palm of the cultured guest or in case the littoral winds should blow aside a curtain—and no paper to be secured. Not a handkerchief or stain of apple core in the brass receptacle by the writer's right foot. No mat of any sort for the elbow to lounge upon. No dustless rectilinear evidence of a pile of notes having been removed and stashed somewhere nearby. (This was because Lupo burned all his notes, all his non-final drafts. There was a fireplace in the room to which all lines drew themselves. The narn of the mantle was slightly rounded, as the wall, as the sooty aperture below the room's single portrait—a daughter or wife or sister of Jove, weary of her work, who drifts to her bedroom and peers listlessly over her shoulder at her scepter abandoned in the hall behind her.)

Chapter Thirty-Five

"You are my dream, Aden. My one dream."

Aden did and did not savor the taste of those words. The taste had the flavor of tullum in it, something of heresy, of oradine—and something of the suggestion that Mirra had infected him, that her insides were turned inside-out inside of him. The idea that he was the fulfillment of Mirra's hopes for herself also made Aden wonder if she had mistaken him for someone else.

He sat in the Annapurna, the Annapurna idled. He was hungry but did not want to eat; the maid, to his knowledge, was still gone; there was no one to know *he* was gone. Mirra was gone. Propelled by sheer melancholy and locked in inertia by sheer wonder at how drunk he might be able to get tonight if he really tried, he and the car drifted down the road and through the gates of his estate. Lake Caroline doled out a roving glow that followed him around its banks then scrambled itself in a logjam of ile and paxwood, with the pricked hine guarding. In the domed headfields, baby janus trees were growing up among bursts of purpureous fitweed that seemed to engulf them in fire. Aden bypassed the Lynch's turnoff and entered a tree tunnel past a stone gateway, a tunnel that half hid one from the openness and the soul jarring sights of the estate's gardens, at the far end of which the indifferent face of his mansion stared out into a sea of gideonbug flashings in the generous sky-bowl basin between it and Aden. The wings of the gideonbugs lapped at the windshield and whipped up the night into a warm pudding of darkness. He nosed the Annapurna into the carriage house, up between a very rusted but well preserved Rubix and the stately Adilante his father had bought during a rare period of material hankering in his forties following the untimely death of Hump Me Jill, a lovely filly who caught the flu, or something, the night before the Tillerman's Test. Aden crept through a side door, burst through the cloakroom and made straight for the bar in the drawing room with a flinching and growing little grin on his face. What he found there made him laugh like a boy. Lording over the bottles with whistling glee, his scant hair wild, was the perfect purgative to Aden's harried mind.

"Opienne! My friend, my brother! Glad you made it old bastard. Come here. Come here."

"I walked from the station."

"There are cabs, you know."

"It was a beautiful, a bracing walk. Nothing has changed here. It is one of the few corners of the ruined world where nothing has changed. Makes me want to ruin it."

"Do it then. Have a drink."

"I was going to keep the bottle, thanks, for my troubles."

"One thing has changed, Etienne."

"Don't look at me like that. She? She. That is not a some-thing having changed. That is a something having hovered and found a new flower. That little filia you were telling me about? You're sober, aren't you?"

"Here, freshen this up. And don't ask me anything. Please, and not about the filia, not about anything. Just tell me about Paris, and Troy."

Chapter Thirty-Six

"Tell me, I feel like a fool. I have never asked anyone this in my life. Tell me I am, tell me I am still beautiful."

"You are still beautiful, beautiful, yes, except you are besmirched. No, please do not move your head. You need to keep it raised."

"Mirror."

"Not quite yet."

"Oh . . . no. Mirror!"

"No, no not yet. This light is not right. Let me be your mirror for now. I will tell you anything you want."

"My bird, my bird! Is it hurt?"

"What bird?"

"I bring a bird wherever I go. Look look. My back."

"Ah, there. Some kind of undifferentiated wingéd thing. Something of a firebird, something of a feathered dorren. Unfinished. No, it is not hurt."

"Orilan, not dorren. Everything is unfinished, you know, you know!"

"Or everything finished."

"I was much more beautiful, before. Before I became old. You should . . . you should have used me for my proper purpose, before I became old. You should have seen me then."

"You are still . . ." (Peter did not want to repeat himself.)

"But I'm all wasted and fucked up."

"You are not that kind of woman, to be used."

"Do not examine me. I know myself better than anyone. I am a head doctor, a curator of the mind, Peter."

"Keep your nose staunched. You will bathe in blood."

"Oh, gloria. That is what we will do."

Lynch tossed in his chair in the next room but did not rise. Theresa Gold tried to rise, and after much collating and counting of limbs did rise, and joining step with step with the care and simplicity of a new nun reciting the rosary she ascended the stairs. Peter followed her and gave manual support, support that she with her free hand continuously and even rapaciously begged lower. She reentered the blinding bathroom, scowled into the mirror, and dropped herself ribbonlike back into the tub as if about to demonstrate a disappearing act. In the water she let swim, if you will allow me the indulgence, vipers of preposterous blood.

"Come come come, please, in with me, in to me."

"I should let you regroup your senses. And then I will take you home."

"I cannot tell you what it is to be sane, what it is to see through the demon blaze in my mind. Do not make me fall down those stairs for you again, please!—I will do it, if only to have you pick me up again. Now come to me, you boy, you fiend."

He went in to Theresa, and she pulled him up onto her chest and he tasted the blood on her chin, her neck, her lips, her face. Now, now! she cried.

"Wait."

"Oh! Oh! Oh! I have never heard or seen a man make such a comment at such a moment!"

She splashed the bloodstained water over the banks of the bath. He bent down and dripped Godwin's poison into her wet ear.

Now the infernal drooping of the jaw, the gritting of the teeth, the darting of the eyes. The watery bulge and crack of her hip bones reached out for him. A woman born in the everrain of an Andaluz sky, cursed with an infinite passion, her eyes hovered dilate in disbelief, they raked back into her skull in resignation. You have seen the monumental scenes of saints burned, hacked, or pulled at with pincers, or all three at once, their faces blurred by the smoke and the outrage at their end—and at the banality of posthumous fame—at whom the onlookers will cant their necks and ripple their lips like curious cartoon birds— they too somehow aware that they are posing for a portrait and will be scowled, or at least looked at, by critics and museum vermin till kingdom come: this was the overture of thankless torture that played upon Theresa's features. She fought him; he resisted; she cried, she spat blood, she beat upon his chest and clawed at her own. She cried that she was losing her mind, losing herself, losing the world in each day that rose and set . . . and when she had a modest hold on his attention she said,

"I don't care if we die. I don't care. I don't care!"

Peter went inside of Theresa Gold. A parched man lifts a glass to his lips and finds it full, finds the spigot bursting, finds the well bubbling and the rope floating in oole, the livestock fat, the harem full, the pages multiplying like cacophones, the lift a parachute, the gates sprung from their hinges and dancing in the prison yard. He lopes home from a ten year war where he ate rotten goon and fleurin, contracted dipsey and nudge, shot at babes, jostled their mothers, called frenzy on the battlements, ripped the hearts from boys—he comes home from war to find his farm recast as a carnival, as a cloud of painted bodies gripping for the sky as shoots of fire. He crawls out into the dead streets and calls for succor, and ten thousand servants come out at once with his bread and wine. And out of the woodworks of taverns and basements, flying off the rooftops to cloud out the clouds, heaping at his feet in treasonous grovel there come a thousand Tatianas with changing faces and ortflower woven in their hair and eyes quaking with joy. He reaches out for one, and the clocks strike every hour at once. There—there it is—the identity that visited Peter's face when he and she found their common mark. And if the thirsty wandering warrior's expression could be turned to that of a girl, such too were the phases of joy that the bathroom mirror observed in Theresa

Gold's verdilant eyes. The two of them felt underneath each other a presence as dure but so far-flung from the touch or sight of flesh that they both came truly to believe that they had perished and were communing as the only warm spirits in the forgotten reaches of time.

In short, it was good.

"We will drown each other."

To the audience of a million flashing lights, Peter drained the tub and dried Theresa head to toe and dressed her in her bloody scrubs and led her (he would have carried her, for ceremony, but he was too weak) to his grandfather's station wagon. She told him her address, then nestled against his chest and fell asleep. He drove through soft, penetrable night, to Ex, to the spired city of Tarne. He idled in front of her house, a domed structure that resembled an igloo on the moon, for a while with her in his arms. He reached to his right—to feel her leaving, to restrain her from leaving—and she was gone. Her voice remained, murmuring all sorts of mischievous things.

Chapter Thirty-Seven

When Peter arrived home, he noticed the moon. Then he slapped his father awake.

"Say something for me, old man."

"What's that kid."

"Say, I haven't the time for quarrels."

"I don't have time for bullshit."

"I mean, say it with the accent."

"I mean, I don't have time for bullshit, kid. Fuck."

"My name is Arthur Godwin, and I haven't the time for quarrels."

"Stop shitting me here. I brought you home a gift. That girl was smart. Half the crap she said made no sense. She was perfect for you. Now fuck off!"

"Now say, I haven't the time nor the patience for your impertinence."

"I don't know what half of that means. Where did she go, after all?"

"She went home. Just move your mouth and recite the words."

"Fuck you kid. Seriously. You should be done messing with my head."

"You've taken the piss on my entire family, for that matter, and I will not go without recompense."

"This is *my* family, kid. I don't know where you get off saying shit like this."

"I'm not saying. You're saying. Come on. You've dishonored my family and I will have satisfaction. I have a design, old man. Come on now. You have dishonorably comported yourself toward the house and name of my family and I will have satisfaction."

"…"

"…"

"You have dis…"

"There you go!"

"Dishonorably discharged your duties."

"Don't tiptoe through it. Rage through it. Storm. And rage."

"Nah, fuck you again. I got you Caroline. Or what's her name. I got you your redemption. Theresa."

"I have a way to get us enough cash for a thousand Theresas and a thousand redemptions."

"I'm not into it, kid. Who's Theresa? Just call Caroline back a thousand times. Who needs money? Your grandfather would have kelped you with his belt by now."

"Then I'll keep Pearlhorn's fortune for myself."

"Pearlhorn's what?"

Lynch had a way of leaning back in his chair that made him look halfway intelligent.

Chapter Thirty-Eight

I did somehow. I overindulged in him. That horse, I am off it. I am past what is. I am only what may be. Or what does not need to be. Or what cannot be.

Mirra walked back down the lane to the ocean. She spoke into the ear of the slaughtered phone, whose severed taproot wagged behind her in the dirt. She was barefoot and nearly bare chested from pulling at her collar. In her free arm there jostled a tray—pickled reed, sitrine and honey, rolls full of yarnfruit jam, some red wine, some sparkling wine in carafes.

What does not need to be. He waits, he does not wait, either way I cannot know. And Lupo could be waiting, or he could be dancing like a grasshopper, like one of his Indians, to skin drums and the skyscraping bonfires of Hell. It strikes me that the whole of life takes place in the realm of darkness. It never does come to light. Things that disappear when shone upon. Darkness itself disappears. I could not see the faces the gods were making before they pulled back the curtain and frowned on me. I cannot see through to the black hole in his heart. These vines—I do not know the vine and how it makes it through the night. I know it is turned towards itself—that its palm is turned towards its face. But forget all this, Mirra. Look there. Just look, Mirra, and when you are satisfied, look away.

She arrived at the beach, she set down the tray, the slaughtered phone dissolved in the night, she held the scale of life and death in one hand, the other hand she reached out to Lupo. He was covered in sweat under the blanket where his heart did the fire dance, Allaire, two three one, and Tipperary, five seven six. With such fervor the heart leapt and capered that he could not sleep without the breaks of life's bridge to nowhere jawing at him. When the waves drew back in fields of glass he fell into consciousness, and the wait for oblivion was a thousand years. If he could, he thought, he would remember this time as one wishes one could remember one's birth. He looked at Mirra. I have stretched phrases over the lives of civilizations, but I cannot span the pure of this face at rest. Let me try with my fingers. There I reach close by her open eye. I will not touch, for fear that my impression will spoil her, fix her in a vain dream cycle, rob her of herself at this so late hour, when all the rest of my life may be oversalted by an incautious hand. To touch, to worship too closely being to destroy, the meniscus of existence this translucent veil, which to impress is to burst. And my reticence to touch her is admission that we are not the same. Do I admit fear?

Chapter Thirty-Nine

"One can only awaken to natural light. Is this not so, Scarlet?"

"It comes too early to awaken. It palls only."

"I did not ask you Katherine darling."

"I haven't run the experiment. My blinds are closed. In case the gods see what goes on in my bedroom."

"And what would they do if they did?"

"They would interrupt it, I think."

"I disagree. My whole life has been thus exposed, without a hitch. Go up to my studio and have a look, after you eat your breakfast."

"I don't know how this racketfruit got so sour."

"It was likely the taste of bile on your lips."

"Foo on you, mother."

"I've seen your work, Dorothy, snuck peeks at it. And I can say you likely sleep or wake so well because you have no issue with the gods' approval."

"That is too charitable of you. My paintings are exclusively blasphemous."

"And so are the gods, Mother."

"I don't know if they would understand the irony."

"But that is why they leave you alone."

"I bribe them with a pastoral scene now and then."

"Or maybe it is a little too charitable to call all your paintings blasphemous. How do you blaspheme a blasphemer? You need innocence for that. But then you would not know what you were doing. So perhaps your work is nothing but run-of-the-mill nectar for Hebe and his pedophiles."

"You are ornery this morning my darling. More than I had hoped."

"I see no profit in existence. There are only the temporary pleasures of eating and gurgitation, and fuck and regret."

"How about ideas, darling. When I was your age I was consumed with Revolution. The savage and suicidal fall of Man, during which he tears the whole world with him into the bloated bowels of Dis."

"And how is that better than being consumed with bodily functions. At least I can feel something. The only feeling to Revolution is the ephemeral illusion of victory."

"But the illusion, the foretaste, the sense that victory is imminent, that keeps the circle turning, Revolution in its way is the experiential religion. Fuck has an end. You can hold it in the hand of your mind almost, so it is no better than a pet, or a shoe. Revolution has no end, it is round the circle forever, it has everything in it, romance, philosophy, war, famine, cannibalism, opera, hymn, shipbuilding, architecture, poetry, painting, pottery, sculpture, and then of course annihilation, and even the annihilation is productive, its heat releases secret seeds from closed cones. Whereas Fuck, what's the difference, the bodily function of excretion, is mundane. Fuck is lazy, it knows not where it is headed. Love on the other hand, that impossible animal, the medusa at the end of the infinite recursion, is another word for Revolution, in that it holds in its nut the hearts of a thousand revolutions, war without end, just until the closing bell—when the moon falls out of the sky, or the sun grows a few miles closer and boils even the bones of the first fish . . . "

"So why did you create me?"

". . . It roused my mind to believe there was some vast chain, some cause and effect, some grand thing."

"What do you believe now, Dorothy?"

"Now, see, a perfectly genteel and respectful question. Katherine should be so shrewd as to ask some, before I expire. What do I believe? I believe my daughter is a gastric ulcer waiting to burst."

"Why inveigh on me, Mother? Bulimia is my revolution. So be it."

"What *do* I believe? Ah...I think I forgot. I believe the Lord is good. Is that what I'm supposed to say?"

"She asked an innocent question."

"The innocent question got its innocent answer. In childhood you believe. In adulthood you act contrary to those beliefs. That is what I believe."

"And then what?"

"From the gravity and collision of the opposites the universe is born again, sordid and beautiful, and we worship her, and defile her, with each step we take, at once trampling her underfoot and coaxing her to a tintinnabulous orgasm, the rain dance we do, baby, babies you have no idea what a joyous thing you are getting into. If you knew, you would not take your youth so lightly."

"This racketfruit is rotten inside."

"All racketfruit are rotten, in their way."

"Have you ever lain with a man for money, Mother?"

"Don't ask her that over breakfast."

"Let's put it this way. I rarely lay with a man who doesn't have any."

"Where did this house come from, these bronze statues, these horses?"

"My art, my dear."

"You never finish anything."

"I get paid beforehand."

"Horse shit."

"And there was Roland."

"You laid with Daddy for money."

"More than once. And more than laid. He was swine, there was no other inducement he could have given me save death."

"So there's no shame in it?"

"Oh there is shame. There is shame in everything. But there is more shame in the not doing of something than in the doing of something, if you ask me."

"But what about the not not doing of a very bad something?"

"Cut it with the badness and goodness, all self-loathing, narcissistic drivel. Depends on how much money, Katherine. You need to be astute about these things."

"And get paid beforehand."

"And get paid beforehand, yes. A promise will often do, if you perform. It will obviously not do if you do not perform. What goes for art goes for the highest and the lowest arts equally. Don't be offended Scarlet, it is only fitting that my child asks the questions she should not ask. But I am getting weary of all this, honestly. I'm going back upstairs for my mid-morning siesta."

Chapter Forty

Mother of Pearlhorn . . . Why did I not think of that before? All clammed up. And What do you Sea? And Who is my Captain in this squall? Do doe dooo. Pool my floundering dream in this packet, and pull the sheet tight. Caravan me homeward through the high desert Millie, Miles, Mermaid, and then fish me straight from the sky. I am mixing my elements, but I am getting somewhere.

Etienne Opienne was thinking, or that was what he thought he was doing. He was one of those who treasures thought without knowing quite what that means—treasures the thought of thought. For better or worse, he maintained his distance from other humans and thus criticism or praise or litmus, except for Aden's, whose he trusted, or felt he could demean and ignore; therefore he had no evidence of whether or not his thoughts were thoughts. Etienne Opienne was thinking and waking up, on a couch in some room he cared not for names—inside, where the light was beginning to bend its eye. To bend? Not exactly. What is it really doing? Every morning I ask myself, and the answer is a blank stare from the sun. The thing itself has no idea what it is doing. Someone should shoot it down.

"I made a room up for you, you know."

Entered Pearlhorn, in robe and loafer smoke, dipping a spoon into germ and curd and meeting both with flimsy lip. The maid was gone. Ianthe.

"I have no use."

"For my hospitality?"

"You haven't made up a room in your life. Where goes my coffee while you're at it."

"I don't know how to work the machine."

"Spoiled bugger."

There was something different about Pearlhorn, apart from the differences that came each day—the slow revelation of his asymmetry through a slight droop in his left eyelid that heightened his look of disgust or concern—something like a sanding and waxing of his cheeks to a new rouge, or a dart of whimsy visited in sleep that made this hangover different from the last one.

"Are you going to tell me what the hell has gotten into you, or am I going to have to guess which of a narrowing and ageing circle of whores has bewitched you now?"

"Mirra Bravo . . . and not only has she bewitched me, she . . . may be coming with us."

"You dreary excuse for a man. I was to be the one coming with us. Mirra Bravo! Give me a piece of that cigarette. Now. Now. Yes, now. Alright. Let me instruct you for a moment. Mirra, as I recall her, is a fine piece of . . . I don't mean to demean her . . . but Santa Theresa is the most vividly striking and delicious of the Lesser Essandrels, and we agreed to summer there—not in the presence of persistent . . . I want to say hangers-on, but I cannot anymore, I must be evermore the gentleman. Even this is despicable, the hold placed on my tongue. And I thought there would be at least a parting kiss from some little white Satan, since all the ones down there are brown, or café con leche, or noisette."

"There may be that Parthian shot yet."

"Aha, so what about this little one, really, the one you spoke of, the estudientka?"

"She is a bit young."

"You want her to yourself."

"That would be unmanly."

"Aha! There goes the smile. You disgusting snake. I believe it was you a week ago that said you'd share her if the opportunity presented itself. Not that that was any necessary enticement to come here. I can get off just fine by myself."

"One last lecture to give at my accursed school. Do you want to sit in?"

"No, thank you. I'd rather sit here. Look, I'll need some light flowing clothing for this trip so that I resemble, to the little diavolas, a mine baron on holiday. And long pants for the little flying diavolos."

"Go upstairs and see what you can find. And pack some for me. I think I started a bag, but it's still empty. I wouldn't know what to put in it. The maid is gone. Ianthe."

Chapter Forty-One

Peter awoke with subhuman difficulty. The palate was scorched, wind scorched or fire scorched, and the tongue had a high desert texture as sand rained onto rock and cemented there as skin. He felt gravity to have fallen off its pedestal and plunged to the museum floor; the severed limbs of gravity ricocheted wildly from the walls. A pitchfork pronged its handle from the central foundry of his mind and punctured his hearing and sight; silence did not sound silent; things did not appear real. He moved, rolled off the bed, crawled to the bathroom, the impossible site of last night's impossible mischief. His eyes were crusted in earthy gypsum, relic, porphyry, networked with toll, lashed with tar. Under the nails and lining the nailbeds and even (he was naked and waiting for the shower to warm and quit screaming) bookending his toenails and filling in the labyrinths that coated his knuckles the rivulets of scarlet black inked and welled. The hairs that waxed faint gold around his chest and down the valley of his stomach and those that wreathed the pubis and battered the legs all carried Lilliputian pirate flags, and those flags that covered his skull (he now stood under the water and watched it happen) melted free and painted at his feet the black fungal face of a cenote proceeding many fathoms down. His reflection hovered at the threshold of the pool, and he bent forward to retrieve it, forward elongating his figure until, with a cold slingshot, his forehead hit the tile of the shower wall and the cavern was washed down the drain. This happened—the pooling and flushing of Theresa's blood—again and again, until the water rinsed a faint glistening yellow, to Peter's mind the color of tosyne flower, the slightly sickly off-white bloomcousin of the lynnde and the hassick, and the one flower he had ever given Godwin, now a century ago in the dugout of the Two Trees ballpark, as a reward or inducement he could not recall— but he did recall the act. He also recalled the flavor of those of Godwin's perfections and imperfections that rated her first to his taste. She had an embracing bowing of her hips and a darkness and stentor and size to her nipples that demanded breasts larger than their bearers; a concavity yet a delicacy to the stomach that conjured a surface softer than water; a nose that did naught more than to indicate the lascivity of the lips; one eye that winked at you and the other that lazed when she smiled, giving the impression that the expression was half-faked. When aroused she tasted of sour bushberries marinated in new wine, not the best bouquet, but an unmistakable one. You could not secure her wrists or hands or feet lest she belt you. And when you pricked her she came alive so apogetically that you were certain she would suffocate from the force of her own operatic seizure. All this topped with hair so fine and near angelic that it seemed glossed from the head of a firebird, when what you really wanted to issue from her skull were coarse spurts of flame. A firebird . . . Theresa. Flame of the farcic chaos of the cream of the thoughts of Theresa Gold.

Peter dried and dressed and descended to find his father back in his chair. Lynch had just called in sick to work. He was going to be fired, but it didn't matter.

"What are you doing."

"What the hell do you think I'm doing. I'm thinking."

"I mean you're not practicing."

"Shitty things like this come to us naturally, kid. There isn't any need to practice."

"Well said. But now I am trebling the tariff."

"Treble? What the hell is a tariff?"

"It's in the script. What, you could have asked last night."

"It was late. I was confused. My sincere apologies."

"Not bad there! But what other surprises do I have to worry about? Do you not know what a queue is? How about a looking glass? A lorry. A bonnet. A quarry."

"I don't know what any of that crap is."

"Your tone, your timbre must be flawless. Otherwise we're dead in the water. Godwin's fugitive father is known to be nineteenth or twentieth in line for the Crown."

"How about this, kid, how about you do this god damn thing yourself. Where the hell are you going?"

"To school. Good luck old man. Treble the fee. We've got nothing to lose now, got it? I can smell the money old man, can't you?"

"I can smell my feet rotting in my socks. Treble?"

Chapter Forty-Two

"Do you love me Scarlet?"

Katherine Godwin lay bleached white naked atop the morning papers. Her hair threw pips and freshets and dromedary drops against a blue and red story of a girl raped then killed for being raped in the subtropical regions of Tide. Godwin had just purged herself in the shower and swooned on the carpet.

"I do love you, Katherine, if love is a thing."

"If you love me, then deliver me from this foul game. Give me a door of deliverance. Give me an idea—an idea—that will dwell in me and not require so much upkeep as all these others. I have ideas that I need to retrofit every morning, only to watch them break down over lunch, and everything is in shambles again by dinner. I need a rock, Scarlet, a rock so solid that if it be broken the whole world will go with it into the vortex and sink to the bottom of the ocean—I need the keystone of my existence."

"You have them inside of you, they may be molten, you need to wait."

"Don't feed me that swill! I need a rock, and you have a whole quarry. My soul is made of clay, like Eva the tempted, the weak, the febrile. I need something cold and unceasing, like hatred, but not just hatred, I cannot hate but myself."

"Then you should convert to a Coot."

"Come with me. You know you love Opienne anyhow."

"Come with you where? I will not be your deliverance."

"This is not deliverance, Scarlet. This is debasement, to a depth from which there is only uptending, there is only recovery and rebirth. Do you have any idea of the theatrics I have decided to pull?"

"I have none. You and Peter keep all sorts of secrets from me. I still don't know what went on the night of the Track Club dance, with the policemen . . ."

Godwin crawled over the carpet and pulled the theatrics on Scarlet.

"Now you see?"

"Jesus Christ."

"You see how irresistible it is, how crowning, how gravitous?"

"You're going to…oh no."

"You see how there is no way out of this?"

"I do. I do. I would not visit that on anyone though. I mean anyone I cared for, and who cared for me. Not ever."

"But at the same time I must."

"And why?"

"It has all gone on too long. Such that Aden and I—we curse one another, renounce one another each moment, and still the tirade of amore rages back like the dread eyes of Athène or

Helène beyond the page of the poem. What we want now is not to love but to kill. The pressure has built too high, so that when he touches me, we will burst, the cycle will be broken, there will be nothing there to take the place of our former desire and angst and self-repression. As Mother would put it, Revolution gives way to the idle world of Fuck. We will die in fact, behind ourselves, so that there will be no reason to inhabit our bodies."

"But what if he actually agrees, Katherine? Then you will have to make good."

"There is no making good from evil."

"You will have to come through with the evil, I mean."

"Let us see what the ghost riders have in store. Peter seems to think Pearlhorn will not relent, that he will recuse himself, that he will not engage in the act, that he will perhaps throw me out the window. I do not think so. I think it is far different when one does not know that I am acting. And acting is as real as any real thing, after all."

"You are starting to jinx this whole thing you know."

"So there is a thing to jinx."

"No, I did not say that."

"You did. There is a meaning in words, Scarlet, and the meaning comes first. Your meaning I could not have mistaken. You are coming with me."

"I give up again. Why am I always giving up? What do you have to gain by all this?"

"The world, Scarlet."

"Through a man's body? Heaven and Hell were once gained through one man's body. Now we've had them for a while, we are bored of them. And the world: I do not care for the world. The world seems to have been left behind for us to choke upon."

"You will one day die choking on air, on nothing. Come on, baby. Let it be something more substantial."

Chapter Forty-Three

Mirra hovered her hand just over Lupo's sleeping nose. One little grasp here, and it seems I could lock the last breath right in him. Lock this last breath, and the fulge of this sunrise too. The philosopher here, and I his handmaid. So many days of servitude in shadow—self surrendered you might say, yes, you might say. Self surrendered, and yet my surrender was accepted. No question of whether the surrender would be appropriate. No question of my genius having a higher pitch, a more fertile and luxuriant croft than his. None knows that mine sits still in a landscape and watches its own visions appear and evanesce unanswered and irreplaceable and without heartbreak, for my genius knows it has no natural terminus. My art is the fire that consumes my canvas. It disdains the boxed form of the letter and line, the measure, the stage, all so contained that my soul's mere whisper would burn a hole in their faces and ceilings and backgrounds. Mere writers, their long fingernails piddling with balls of dried pus harvested from their ears, yellow crusts hanging at their nostrils, litter clawing at their eyes, eyes that waver from nearsightedness, the only colors of their palate black and white . . . Just a pinch and a stifle, and he will not overcome—but why do I feel always that someone is watching when I do my highest desire? Seabirds, parade of sand swallows turn away! Jakepeppers turn away! Sun and moon turn away! Here only I loom. Loom and what? I tire. All this ducking and hiding renders me unfit to attack when the good is to be gotten. And the smoke of my own fire comes and lashes at my face and occludes the truth I just now thought was inviolable. Too clear a vision, he says, was my downfall. I saw my own image written in the skies and became fixed with it—so he explains my fascination with him, his fascination with me. He forgets, so easily he forgets, that in that blow he delivered to my eye he admitted I had touched him to the deep. There is no one watching. There is never anyone watching. Here was the place: here will be the place.

"Fuck!"

She dropped back into the sand and swaddled herself in her blanket.

I cannot do it. Cannot cannot. Cannot cannot. The unrepeatable I cannot do. And so I am like music. Music I am like. Music. It does naught but repeat, because music is the orbit of the orbs, my eyes, my eyes, it is all contained in knots and weaves inside the instrument that waits for its composer and player, and its tones come alive when they come around again and meet their sisters, the knot and weave distend. So thus I would not kill lest I could kill again the same. I would kill God only, or some theoretical spirit whose dregs do not spill completely out when you tip him over. The lines of Whitson: *I alike to Pilate when he thought / let them have the King, I know that He / cannot in fact die, poor god of a thing.*

I cannot do it because I want this man to suffer longer and therefore to know more—to stand outside the palace vestibule of his life, the gentle rain of the early morning tickling his cheeks and forming quicksilver galaxies on his eyelashes, and bid adieu to the spirits that danced that long evening of his life until he has shaken each last ghostly hand. Now his arm swings mechanically in the ether, and the maid, the only one left inside, little Mirra, little I, is casting him a pitiful stare from atop a mountain of spent and shattered wine glasses and bottles, besmirched napkins, funereal tablecloths over funereal tables, and unevenly burned candelabra holding torches of botched wax.

Chapter Forty-Four

Peter Senior was practicing for a dance on the criftpad of glory. Look at me, he said to himself in the mirror, why shouldn't I win this round? I a boxer, a swimmer, a jumper, a field goal kicker— I will shave my moustache for this. He should not hear it bristle in the receiver when I rob him. I will shave my moustache. I should trim my privates for it too, to mark the occasion. Give it a haircut. If I had curlers I would give it a perm.

"Jesus what a press. What a cram. What a fucking unbelievable jam."

(Lynch had looked up the meaning of treble.)

He abluted profusely, was hungry and tired, and abluted again. On the toilet he reviewed his lines. Certain of them did not sit with him; he changed them, then changed them back; changed them and back again. They did not sit well because he did not know what they meant, and whole exchanges went barren on his tongue. He tried to remember how Peter had instructed him—to hold his pitch high or low, or was it permitted to sound sinister, evil, or was it permitted to sound clever, or was it permitted to sound offended. Pearlhorn presented a challenge. The man was Lynch's superior in discretion, in humility, in silence. Lynch had never heard the man nor his father waste a word. Or was it that they would not waste a word on him. He thought it more likely that the men would not waste a word on him—or that Pearlhorn did not know how to speak to low characters, only Ex men and Tineburg women with starched collars and horses that they kept for the sole purpose of having their portraits painted (with, or upon, a horse). And perhaps Pearlhorn would as of right pay no mind to the demands of some ghostly Roland Godwin, who may too occupy some inferior unspoken rank. Lynch had not the slightest whiff of Pearlhorn's wishboning of his wife, nor that Pearlhorn weekly said things to Mirra that you do not say, things having to do with the slashing of gullets and the shedding and intermixing of bloods. Nor had he heard of Aden's recurring dream of a party where Mirra was dying of black pall in a back room but persisted in sending flowers out to him in the hands of a waitress who would not have it any other way and would not let him in; his other of drowning at sea but not dying, and he haunted the bottomless underwater caverns a breathless homunculus searching for Mirra in the form of a sea-strophe; his still other dream of falling face first in a car with her over a precipice and staring through the proliferate veins of the blood-bespattered windshield, unable to turn his paralyzed neck to see what state Mirra's crushed body had assumed. He did not know that Aden had fears and habits that not even you and I, for want of resources, can get into—that he stood in the kitchen lost for three or four hours at a time, not thinking and not meditating, just lost; that he twitched and seized without notice in his sleep and clawed for a being he knew did not exist but whom he named Cyderia or Cimmbalic or Sybille and whose hair he could feel on the pillow entwined with his and mixed up with the maid's; that the maid was gone; that Aden cracked up from the changing of seasons and could not endure in spring all the heightpool and crift in his fields and would tell the men to shave them out for surfeit of bloom, but would be tempted to grope and gape through the pile of clippings when no one was at hand. None of these things had Lynch heard or seen, so to him, the man Pearlhorn did not dream. He read the international papers in four languages. He knew the price of sternfruit in East Roll, and the tariff on fine Aliman cigars in Yarnfeer; he knew which way the winds blew out of Dearside on a Wednesday at Whitsuntide, and could sail a schooner across the Channel shorthanded; he knew the names of the trees and bushes and grasses and birds and howlers and seekers in the Irhis country—and beyond; he knew the names and faces of all the dead and living kings and queens of Acerrimus and could recite their tastes in wine, marmalade, bedtime lore, and hunting prey. He could swim across the Bleak River if he wanted to. He knew how to fly a Raidscour Fifty by instruments and once took the reins from a pilot when the latter had a heart attack midway between Fioretown and Bizarre Point. He landed the plane like a feather and saved one hundred seven lives—and with a delicate hand to the pilot's temple diagnosed the heart attack as acid reflux while taxying to the gate. He could sound out the alphabet in pairs from the middle, and play sixteen chess games at once, blindfolded, by feel. Lynch's Pearlhorn did not throw up his hands when cornered by bears or detectives—nor did he let himself be thrown into disarray and delirium by the thought of distillate coating the downy thigh of a schoolgirl. Lynch lay down paralyzed. He cut his nails, twice, and impulsively filed them with Mirra's file. He descended and made some more coffee and filled the living room with smoke. A paxwood clock that he seemed not to have noticed for years chattered on the wall. He threw the script down on the table. Did he dare pick it up again?

Chapter Forty-Five

"A far more eloquent version of this lecture was delivered by Professor Charles Whitson at Ex, when I was his student, and later in his famous monograph, *Josfrende In Exile.* You will forgive me my own dim understanding of some of the more subtle details, but the argument runs something like this. Remember the scene when Orelia takes the necklace from King Fear's throat and hangs it on her own, and meditates on the meaning of her coronation? Let us read the lines, and please for the arcane elements, jade, barnsows, et cetera, see the glosses. *And with this amulet gold and jade / I mortify the dreary ghost / That thought an ethereal princess made / From mindless clay by heaven's smoke.* What is Orelia saying? No no, hands down, I'm not supposed to do this but I will tell you what she is saying. The heroine unchains the hero, that much is for sure. She unchains him and he *Leaps and scours the ground for food / As a barnsow sordid and rude.* If Fear is unchained and put wild, then Orelia is now somehow chained—chained to what? What is in a title or a rank, and what, exactly, is the title Orelia assumes? Is it the weight of royalty that drives Fear to his undoing, and the taking of the amulet is a passing of that dread torch, or is it his uncloaking, the unburdening of that royalty that exposes or brings on the beast beneath all that ceremony? We should not say both, because Josfrende is not a copout. We should say one, and I say the one is the first one. By this point in the play, Fear is beyond mad—he has been mad from the beginning—and so it cannot be that the removal of the title that drove him here has anything to do with it. If he were not mad already, Orelia would not have occasion to demote him and assume the throne. And listen to Orelia as she mocks God for thinking that he made an *ethereal princess* from *mindless clay* by, we must assume, mere smoke and mirrors. Airy—light—mindless—she is none of these things; she, now, carrier of the royal amulet, is burdened with the land and the subjects, the glory and the power, influence you could say beyond that of God who diddles about in Paradise, beyond that of any spirit or thing. Power over life and death: like a cancer it will drive her mad too, it will sow her undoing, since now the invading armies know whom to kill. They see the divested Fear rambling on the heath out of his mind and they do not care to waste steel on his life. It is Orelia they are after now. The threat of high power and high murder follows the amulet. Orelia's last words: *And when I have breathed my unblessed last / Cut this chain from my neck of ashen snow / So that my soul may seek the skyward glow.* Power, kingdom, ownership, influence are the soul's solitary confinement.

"Or are they? How much did a twenty-six year old amateur playwright know of the curse that followed the queen that perched on other people's coins? Was it royalty that killed Orelia, or was it the fact that when she slipped the amulet over her neck, she became the protagonist—and the protagonist in a tragedy must die—there is no other way about it? The title of hero or heroine is the most ephemeral.

"Reminds me of those lines of Whitson which I hope you will retrace one day on your own. He wrote them on a sailing ship in the mid Flange after losing his third wife to pneumonia. *An artist is no hero but a wayfarer / who trods the glacial memory, the icy clods / Of sea glass and chimerical wreck / That imprison Orelia's mythic neck.*"

Aden stood by the door and shook hands. The mass of students shuffled by and wished him well; some were sobbing, the girls. He did not see them. The wind flowed out of him in final relief and lassitude, and he was removed from the scene to his office, where he vanished behind his desk. Years passed. He had grown stouter by the villagers' eyes, the villagers in a hill town above an alpine lake numb cold like Whitson's glacial memory. Around the lake ran a faint vermilion crushed stone path that he walked in the mornings with his sheepherdess and her child. The three spoke to one another in broken Latin and perfect Italian; each time they walked they found new words to describe the crooked breeze, the walls of the fortress, the waiting trees. The tender undersides of their chins and the roofs of their mouths grew bronze from the lake's reflections that followed them everywhere, to each a sun...

"I will come, but not alone."

"..."

Aden opened his eyes. There was a voice in the room, a bell's late howl, a voice. It told him,

"Not alone."

And the source sat so close to him on his desk that he could feel the breath coming off her, breath of try, of work, of the lower strata of the flesh that precipitate in struggle and war, flight, slavery, the steps of the gallows. Her loafered feet visibly shook. Scarlet's hands framed Godwin's face, and one fished back the strays from Godwin's forehead and couched them just behind Godwin's ear. Scarlet whispered,

"Mercy . . . "

. . . into that ear and looked sidewise at him from Godwin's temple. Her hand traveled down the center of Godwin's chest, and came to rest on her lap. Scarlet said again,

"Mercy."

Godwin gazed inscrutable down at her teacher. She winced; Scarlet's words had begun to tickle her; she pulled tight Scarlet's head to her collar, where it rested. Scarlet closed her eyes.

"I will come to your little salon tonight, but I need a protector. Protectress, I mean."

"Opienne and I are readying to leave. There are preparations to be made. I do not know now. I'm sorry."

"He shares your desire to withdraw from all this?"

"He does. He has always been withdrawn."

"And when?"

"At first light tomorrow. I would rather be rested."

"And the airline?"

"My pilot."

"Private. The itinerary?"

"Hop to Creolis to refuel and then to Santa Theresa."

"Hotel?"

"There are no hotels to my knowledge in Santa Theresa proper."

"The address of the house."

"60 meters west of the intersection of the roads Tilia and Gregoria, Frutas Secas, La Virgen de Guadaloupe, Santa Theresa."

"Yours?"

"Mine."

"Bedrooms?"

"Two, but I only need one. And he one."

"Water?"

"Cistern."

"The brand of the faucets."

"Come on."

"..."

"..."

"So you are not bound to leave tomorrow."

"I am never bound, Miss Godwin."

"You said it, not I."

Aden pushed his chair back from the desk and averted his eyes to the blank face of the sky and the weeping crown of the splitleaf remus tree, very rare, that set off the beyonds and wept over the tepid stone of the garden walls and sipped the rippled surface of the fountain into which Bellacitta trickled the contents of her urn. In his sightscape lingered a purple concavity in the shape of two idols demanding worship and even penance. He turned back to the girls; they filled the outlines of those idols and made them burgeon and flow.

"Tonight is just not…"

Scarlet, awakened on Godwin's shoulder from dark reverie to darker, all revealed in her gaze in which swam felonious and other monstrous nocturns, a gaze that told what Godwin could not tell so silently and succinctly—it was Scarlet who silently interrupted him. Now Godwin,

"There is never a good time for what we are about to do, Mister Pearlhorn. Put off your eternity of leisure and peace for a moment. And I am thinking of those lines of Whitson, the ones that go, how do they go?"

"Mercy."

"*I was taken to a scarlet bird that sings / The very lines of which his master thinks / I stepped close in and met his ebon eye / He said, 'your wings are clipped, you cannot fly.'*"

"Very good, Miss Godwin, but I don't know if the next line agrees with your meaning, the one that goes…"

"*And then the voice from where my heart should beat: / I need no wings but loft of entropy.*"

"Yes, that one."

"I think it agrees just fine."

Godwin's open lips stayed in waiting. Pearlhorn perched and lingered at those gates and looked around him. The shepherdess and her child descended into the water. They brought with them the landscape bloated and choked with green and blue, punctuated by boulder cliffs giving off into the perfect softness of the valley. Night descended. A flower exploded in the moonlight. The lake shone constellations at the heart of the earth. Goodbye, he murmured. Goodbye, goodbye.

Chapter Forty-Six

"Life did not begin in a place utterly devoid of life. Or you can say that the place devoid of life, the sky, at one time was full and emptied itself on the earth. Or you can say that what we see as a duration of life is an interlude between two lives, each without end. Now, if you cannot pin down your frame of reference, how can you say anything for sure about the finer details?"

"If we were always so skeptical we would never speak, my dear Mirra."

"You spent the greater part of yesterday telling me of myself—through the lens of a character I myself invented. I am to you, you say, the negative image of my own fantasy—whom I vaguely remember not as myself but as someone or something to care for, like a zaichik—nor do I remember him taking days off, besides his occasional naps, when I could enjoy my meals or books or walks without fear of interruption. There was never a Mirrita in the sky—that is your invention, a vestiga of the innocent daughter you lost when she threw herself into the abyss."

"I did not mean to say that there was a 'you' floating in the sky in fact. There are simply certain thoughts that can only be expressed through metaphor, which to say straightaway would deflate them. Take Burnish. Why did he write *The Rensellar* instead of simply stating to his readers that the world is a random gathering of energy without evolutionary tendency? There is something in the experience of the idea. And there is something in the way you have experienced yourself. I cannot say it in a word—how your steps are taken as if you feel the air to be a canvas, as if you feel yourself to be initiating your own foreshadow. Your gaze as if you are peering through a mirrored maze at a scrambled image of the minotaur inside, and challenging him to a battle of wills, or a corrida through the bushes, knowing you will lose—and win. The victor and the vanquished hover there. That is why I see you as a dual phenomenon, one here on earth, one up in the outer space of your mind like a kite, where there is no gravity and thus no meaningful control. And you have her by an increasingly fraying string. This not meant as an insult to you but more of a marvel, to me."

Calm, hatted bodies moved among the vines in the background, counting and fondling the fruits. Mirra fell and rose through the air on long period in a hammock and gave herself momentum by pressing on the stone with one hand and smoking with the other, a confluence of motions, back and forth, in and out, that settled her breakfast on the one hand and pushed off surfeit on the other. She had an idea in mind for a painting of a figure of whom neither the age nor sex could be ascertained. An ancient child god of sorts. She would paint the thing, set it on fire, paint it again, and that would occupy her until sundown, when it would be permitted to stop painting, for the colors would have bled from the landscape and the mind. Mirra turned her cheek against the weave of the hammock and framed Lupo in her gaze. He was outfitted in silver grey linen that caused his whole dreary outline, taut ribboned cheeks and polished, increasingly paling pate to blend in with the sea scorched clapboard behind him. His elaborately framed and decorated eyes were cast down at a pipe he was packing.

"You're supposed to be dying."

"I've always been dying. To give up a pipe is far worse."

"And what of your tearful note, my Burnish."

"It was you who just said that life was a mere interlude."

"I did not say mere, I said interlude. And your Burnish did his best work during his interludes—when he was not thinking about the beginning or the end or the point of the thing, when he was not thinking at all. Laloila called her only piano studies, composed just before her prescribed death and never played by their creator's hand, and each one a work of fancy surpassing Dorin, Interludes. The Interlude, filmed in San Marco by Goodman and Traiser, covers five generations of a family of gypsies who, tragically you might say, find their way back into society at the end. The simple commonality, or one of them, between these durations being their circular quality, but that is not all."

"No, that is not all."

"Speaking of circular quality, how big is this hole you have, in your heart?"

"The size of a baby's fingernail."

"To think, that is your undoing."

Mirra stumbled off the terrace and into the sunlight, where a loud hatchback dart followed her, leaving Lupo in a bit of precious silence. The silence began to cloy; the scripters in the trees filled it up; he reached for a book; there was none there. Then Mirra returned with a revolver the size of an adolescent road piper.

"What do you think of this thing."

"I think we have no beasts big enough for it."

"Would you shoot yourself with it?"

"I would not."

"And why."

"It's a cannon. I would leave no trace of myself. It is also, by the by, an antique. Look at that detail there. The Western Flinch, that bird, and so too the gun. Where did you find this?"

"On the desk of my loved one, in a case almost as beautiful as the weapon itself. I took it when I left. He is a poet. A teacher and a poet."

"Thank gods you have strayed from that blackguard of a carpenter."

"My loved one—he writes of nothing but death. He lusts after it more than he lusts after me, only somehow he prefers to be alive for the lusting. He has other guns, rifles, shotguns, little pistolets, but he only shoots himself with this one."

"Shoots himself. He makes a habit of it. Is he a ghost?"

"He sets up mirrors in the yard and duels with them. He has no other means of bravery. Someday, I know, he will in fact kill himself dead. He will tire of repetition, he will run out of lines, and his image itself will stall."

"And you imagine he will not think of another way to destroy himself? This gun must be one of a pair, you know, as the tide warriors of lower Casanova would not be caught dead without armament."

"He is no tide warrior nor Casanova. He is your brother. Just as that centavo hole in your heart is filled by my presence, he cannot miscarry now, with me away. I am the pendulum that swings between your souls."

"So why should you take the gun, a mere menace to the bounds of the body?"

"My fear, fear and desperation, helplessness and haste, lassitude of faith."

She wiped the silt and dust off the gun with the tails of her shirt, first white as a veil or matrimonial sheet, now dirty as the two used, so she thought, and buried the thing anew in the garden. Lupo relit his pipe and found his book. When he looked up, Mirra was folded in the hammock with a sheet of fine linen propped up against a broad picture book on the unexplored islands of Eastman Sound, and a palate of watercolors weeping onto her lap like so many shipwrecked brides. She painted one portrait—of Lupo in inimitable sky, with a flourwood walking stick in his hand topped with some tusk or other and gleaming. A dreary lapel of his morning coat hung from his chest where the heart should be. The eyes were the ones she saw, instruments of weightlessness and deliverance. She went out on the lawn and burned the thing up, then painted it again.

Chapter Forty-Seven

The three, Katherine, Scarlet, and Peter Junior, were hung up in the paxwood like pulses in the cosmos, somewhere near fifty paces from the ground, where it had been convenient to triangulate themselves and each other atop a thatched roof of branches. Katherine fell early from the tangle of limbs and impaled herself on the amber daggers of a lower tier. One took blood from her thigh.

"A dome carapace of blood on my leg. Our lifeblood is our deathblood. Am I the only being in the universe that finds this odd."

"Too preachy, Katherine, I'm trying to sleep. Please meditate, or something."

"Yes, too. What he said. I performed for you today Katherine, twice, I performed flawlessly, and I would not have if I had foreseen that your philosophizing would cut dry my bliss."

"You're not paying attention. Last night they murdered the president of Rialto. Squads are in the streets. Ancient treasures have been torn and overturned. The tomb of Gaius Tereus Septus Mixtus, or whatever his name was, has been opened. And you speak to me of meditation and bliss. I speak of blood, the only thing."

"That business in Rialto is no more real to me than if you stabbed a stuffed elephant in Doremus and called in my murder.

"But there is no anchor to this confusion, my dear Peter, to lend weight to your metaphor. There is only the bloodflow of tragedy in life. I hear a song in my head, repeating, repeating as if I were born with a music box inside of me. The song's words I cannot make out, because they are so familiar, they are as my own face weighing on itself, and I do not have the proper mirror to tease out the shape, the lyric of the song. Yet sometimes I do hear it, in dreams Peter, in dreams, and I can . . . "

She painted the blood wide and wider on her thigh, and began to paint on her face bloody moustache, blood eyebrows, blood rouge to the waxen cheeks, blood beard, blood chops, then joined the elements to form a blood mask. She squeezed the wound to reinvigorate the palate. Now. Blood moccasins, blood pudding, blood halo to her pelvis, blood handlebars to her chest.

" . . . I can see the music in dreams, it takes the shape of a pendulum. You might say just now, aha yes, it is a metronome turned on its head, keeping the meter of the tune. It swings and returns, and pauses, and swings and returns and pauses— so it tells the story of the song, which ends and repeats, ends and repeats, and even pauses, if you will, at its two terminals, if you think of it being played backwards. But what of time returning? How can a pendulum represent time itself, which we always think of as a continuum, with ineluctable leavings behind of what is said to have come before? I say it can, for life, and therefore time is a foray into a horseshoe magnet whose two terminals kiss at death. The tragic cycle is the only cycle. Comedy is only half the story, and note that all comedies end in marriage—the high point—from which there is only descent."

"You should cut yourself again."

"But that's not what I mean, I mean that the song the pendulum represents, the one I keep hearing, is the death knell, my own, and it is a remembered song, for my death is both ahead of me and behind me, I can taste my death as an aftertaste on my palate, just as I taste this blood. My death is so near, all I need to do is fuck my way into it. Just as I was made, I will unmake myself."

"You have already tortured us both with this idea, you monster, you fiend. I am not touching you again, if to touch be to kill. Go to your white knight Pearlhorn, he will defenestrate you, as that seems to be the way you want to die, like a Pope, like a woman of God, God's messenger, his midwife, his whore."

"And now my bliss is soiled with the sight of you covered in blood like an island savage from the accounts of De Los Reyes. This whole tree smells of heavy metals, the last elements left in your raped body."

"I can wipe it off, Scarlet baby. I can wipe it off."

"Don't call me baby. Where is Rialto, by the way? I hate you so much."

"What ever happened to love, Scarlet baby? You use us like little slaves, me and Peter, your two acolytes, your altar boy and girl. Wait and see what happens when we go. You will rot away in regret."

"Love's dead, baby. We are living proof."

"Just breathe."

"My blood itself is thirsty. It needs renewal. I need to turn inside out but cannot. I have tried so many times and failed…"

"Breathe Scarlet."

"…"

"Breathe! Breathe woman. It is akin to turning a woman into a man. Imbuing her with the prey. There we go. She's free."

"Free!"

Shouted Scarlet. She tottered out naked to the elastic middle of a branch and howled at the armies, the fortresses, the mountain peaks, the fallen, and at Peter, who lay wasted at the hinge of the branch. A moment later, shivering and chained by gravity and fearing falling, she examined what had taken rest on Katherine Godwin's thigh. The curiosity of the wound and the work of art it had engendered narrowed and silenced her attentions, and she pushed the blood to and fro with her fingers, making first a figure eight, now a figurine, added wings, horns, scepter, now back to the spring of blood, drank it up, and watched the tide pool fill again.

Chapter Forty-Eight

Aden left Marywood early and without saying his goodbyes. He left out a back door, one of many low hatches originally cut in the fieldstone archways of the recommissioned mansion for the passage of servants and deliveries of Enseen river fish gleaming on beds of ice, and he disappeared into the shade of a court-yard formed by the walls of the mansion, the outer wall of the garden, and a humpback rock formation in whose cradle the Annapurna lay while he worked. It was about noon. Flows of spark hovered in the air among icculan spruce, sternfruit trees, spent petals of crift that agitated on the whirlpools of air and paused in their quiet hearts. I would merge, he narrated to him-self, I would merge with this picture, say, as a bed of earth to drink the puddles of rain and silt the grass and give the trees their due of ordinary life while they rise, ordinary rest when they fall, no mind to the sky that ignores and demurs to re-ceive, no mind to the middle space that changes, no mind at all. I would, and I will descend, just not now, but why then, and how, and when, and how? He drove, the engine and his mind brewed slow. He idled down the Marywood drive and into the town. Let me go home to Opienne. Let me please go home to Opienne and the bottle, any bottle, a bottle of water even! But it is too early and I am too raw inside, too alone to consent to even epidermal contact with laughter. Let me look in at the bakery, just look in, though knowing that when I look in, the sought one will not be there, not there today, not there tomorrow, never there in eternity even when she is there, a dream that flickers and sings and is not seen but for when one is helpless to seize her. Drive, drive, and knowing she is not there, I starve—I starve for hunger itself it must be, or for vacuity—I want to be cut open.

He arrived at the bakery.

The window, the window! A light, perhaps? A presence? No, no one is here but reflections of others looking in too, looking in at the diorama, the metals, the copper mazes that hang in the ceiling, the drowsy machinery of Mirra's soul. How superfluous other people are, not to mention their reflections—my body aches with them—how vile and how inopportune—but not even vile: if they were vile I would know what to do with them, but here I have this blank stare in me towards the world entire, except for one. Which one?

He parked in the street and went down an alleyway barely wide enough for the light to reach its ground and into the odenrome-walled sanctuary in back of the bakery, where a mat of trintalia gauzily veiled the nakedness of the numis stone. There was a cast iron chair. He sat down. His lips trembled and distorted themselves into aquarian shapes. It was not the first time he had spoken to the back wall of Mirra's bakery. It was the first time that he had asked the back wall of Mirra's bakery for permission. All the other encounters had involved confessions and apologies.

"Where do I begin?"

He lit a cigarette, symbolically.

"Mirra, I've known you for many years, I have grown up, at least grown out of my youth, in you, as I might have done in the arms of a god if I had been alone; yet now I feel that I need to perish somehow before I attain you fully, as the nameless one demanded, before I abolished him in your favor—he who in his divine necrophilia wanted to be spoon-fed my insides in proof of his own existence, and if such a being existed, how could he be so consumed with greed, if he were not in fact the sun itself, and the sun is mute, mute!—

"I feel I need to carve a hole in my chest where the divine emanation, if it does hide somewhere, hides, and let it out. I need to let the shepherdess out. The shepherdess, incidentally, is you, but not only you. It is the maid, Ianthe. I love her because she does not love me. And the shepherdess is a hundred others. She is all those who have come before Godwin, and then she is Godwin as well—she has every face I have ever wanted to possess, she is interminably lost and nameless and yet possessing all names. That is a large part of the trouble. The impressionistic, nay the cubist reality of myself.

"I try to waive goodbye to the shepherdess, yet she returns, and I do not know who she is, moment to moment. Why must there be a she? Why cannot there be simply an I? I don't know, I do not want to know. Life is a parade of darknesses, the repeated discovery of a nameless, empty womb. Now that I've set forth the trouble, the challenge, I hope we can discuss the subject of my coming to your bakery in your absence. You see . . . "

" . . . " (The bakery did not interrupt him; he simply found that his cigarette had withered away.)

"You see, in cases such as this one we've entered into—in bondages, or whatever you might want to call them, long term speculative assignations, there ought to be some kind of grandfather clause, whereby the legitimate, meaning the unquestionable and unexorcisable attachments of the partners are brought into the mix, whether they be younger girls, housekeepers, cousins, sisters, mothers, even mothers, why not, and especially oneself . . . "

" . . . " (The bakery was not having it, at least not exactly this way.)

"Start again. Look. There comes a time in a certain sort of human's life when affection, or what is to be called affection, or desire, the evolutionary tilt towards multiplication, is not the end-all of his existence. Especially for the artist, things such as symmetry, for instance, come into play. Take a hypothetical woman: she has blue eyes, and so do I—she has hair close to white, and so do I, albeit for different reasons—and we both have a reckless disregard for all things but the immaterial, the poetic. Even the immaterial she does not regard too highly. Whereas you have this attachment to, this obsession with physicality, with the way things appear—and in your watercolor combinations you record that obsession, in the cooked combinations of this bakery you purvey that obsession. Contrast that with me, who has not eaten for days in your absence, and Godwin, for example, who I know vomits up every last shred of solidity she ingests. Godwin and I fantasize about starving ourselves to death, emptying ourselves out. While our skin hews close to our bones, yours floats over yours, airy and full like whipped milk. There is symmetry, and there are poets other than Whitson, who is my poet to begin with—he is my poet, you borrowed him—and he must be Godwin's too, or else she would never have mentioned that mind-reading bird . . . some ghostly equation has taken shape."

". . . " (The bakery showed signs of dismay and impatience in its greying cheeks. It knew something was afoot.)

"I can always do better. You see I dislike this, in a way, this appeal you have to a higher being, your other Mirra, your Cerulea, up there in the outer known, higher beings being higher in lower ways than the lofted mind might see them at first. My ears writhe at your worn invocation of the ethereal: I see the sky in your eyes, our love is written in the sky, we will meet again in the sky, the clouds are floating, the night is freckled—and though I would restrain myself from making my argument negatively, anything a mediocre mind finds flawless I must reject offhand. Between the road and sky is my domain, I ride that razor's edge of the horizon that eludes human reckoning, it being highest in every point we see, and lowest in all those we don't. Perhaps that is my curse."

". . . " (The bakery's attention span was due to expire.)

"I know, I know. I have no authority to judge what is high and low, and where the two are divided. But I must speak of something nonetheless."

Aden Pearlhorn lit himself another cigarette. He breathed a few times without saying anything, even to himself—a durée of double-silence that had not occurred since his fifteenth year, when he had gizzarded himself with a branch while skiing a tight line of midlothian spruces at Aufherbum. (He was electrically awakened aboard the rescuing chopper, a Whirlibird 500 hired by Aden's "rich uncle," a silks baron from Rugerfinn who had taken the entire family to the Carrefors as cover for his adulterous stalking of the Bonhamptin starlet Nell Peace.) Then Pearlhorn stood, reached out his hands as if to create some sort of triple-silence, and offered the wall a large sum of money, a sum so despicably large it would nearly turn a human into another species of being, placed in trust for the benefit of Mirra Bravo and her descendants, or thrown by the handful at her disapproving feet until she was buried in it, in exchange for permission to—and I'll let him say it—

" . . . die inside of Katherine Godwin and leave my last and best to rot, because what they call true love is damned and cannot be saved."

Waves of disgust climbed his gullet and exploded against the crescent littoral of his skull. The bakery itself took umbrage and got clean up off its foundations and staggered about its lot back and forth, hunched over like a very fat beached sea creature thrown into a daze by its own fabulous heft. It peered over its eaves at Pearlhorn as it swayed, its dormered eyes drooped in dismay and created a space of time in which Pearlhorn might recant. At exhaustive length it sat back down upon its haunches, scratched its head, and opened its hands in a gesture admitting relent. Pearlhorn bent over between his knees and wretched in a low moan again and again: nothing came out. He had not eaten since the morning; the maid was gone.

Chapter Forty-Nine

Etienne Opienne was having a pleasant day. Any amount of travel, even a bicycle ride with his illegitimate son, would normally throw him off course for months, but travel to Pearlhorn's place was an exception. Two Trees, the estate not the town (he was not one for towns) fit neatly in his hierarchy of sensory achievements next to, or even on top of, Forchon, the undulate keep of spine conifers in the valley of Geed, pronounced Good, in Baad Baad, pronounced Bad Bad, near Opienne's childhood home. Opienne reclined on the couch, one of six or eight in the drawing room, and he moved to another each few moments or so, to freshen his view and provide occasion for the freshening of his drink. Out the parsed glass of the terrace doors, a face of purple clouds hung inexplicably in the sky. Opienne's gaze kept flitting from the empty page: why not take a walk out to the point where he could touch that face?

He walked outside. Alas, he would never reach the chin of those clouds in this lifetime. He would have to wait until death. Or longer. He returned to the drawing room and began to write. The process was painful, like giving birth to a hydra through one's asshole. I translate, horribly:

I would ask to bow
In a monkish manner
And please to free myself,
When I am finished,
To go crablike,
From mountains to molehill
And gorge myself on your depths.
(Je veux me joindre la tête aux pieds
Dans le mode d'un moine
Et s'il vous plaît me libérer
Quand je suis ramper fini
dans le mode d'un crabe
De tumuli à taupinière
et me gaver sur votre cul de sac.)

He read the poem until it was funny, laughed derisively himself to tears, tore it up, and started again, wrote it over, tore it up again. This was his mode, that of a crab, he sidled up to a poem and over it again and again, until there remained nothing but dirty feet on the page, tags to remind him who he was, and what he was doing. Who was he? He was the Pied Piper, hooting and tooting the world into carnal abysmum. What was he doing? He hoped to attract like-minded little girls, dark or light or café, he did not care, to the far-flung and langor-lacquered shores of Santa Theresa by publishing something profane in the politica-literary magazine *Hangman* (or *Canplayer Weekly* would do) and noting his new residence in the by-line. He would prevail upon

Pearlhorn to dub him the "Pearlhorn Poet-In-Residence," or some such tosh, to cast upon his pitiful situation a patrician glow. Etienne pulled on his beard. Then,

"Aiiiiiiihhhhhhhhgggggggrrr."

He started at a flare of shrill shot through the napping air and off the terrible narn and numis of the house that flared so suddenly that it seemed to come before itself. Etienne fell apart, his whole mind shattered. He groped dizzily and blindly into the dead garden of vase, lamp, and telephone on the table next to him. Up came the receiver, dropped down just as soon, and screamed again in close succession. He repeated the motion, and now his eyes began again to pray forth beyond the image advertised in the windowed doors to the terrace and into its changing and shining source.

"A walk anywhere would do."

he said. It rang again.

"This is Opienne."

"You French bastard, why will you not talk to me?"

"Because I do not wish to."

"You amnesiacal rot."

"Speak for yourself, you oenomaniacal shrew."

"Where is my groom?"

"Groom? It is true then! I want to kill myself."

"Do you think the marriage is useless?"

"Everything is useless. You might as well marry."

"Just pass on a message for me?"

"Depends on the message. I don't remember names, dates, places, or anything having to do with the future. The future is not memorable by its nature."

"The music of reality does not answer to the strings. It is the other way round."

"As you wish; you have lost me."

"Very good Etienne."

" . . . "

" . . . "

"Mirra. Are you going to speak?"

"What kind of message should I send him? I didn't have one to begin with."

"Well . . . to start you could tell him you're not going through with it. That you will elope with me instead."

"That would not do."

"You think he cares one way or the other?"

"No offense to you, Etienne. I would simply like to be more cryptic."

"Then tell him you've jumped off a cliff."

"I've already faked suicide. He faked his own right after. For three weeks we were dead. Think of that."

"What made you come back to life?"

"Boredom with being dead."

"I can see that."

"Tell him he should suicide his works of art, he should throw away his poems as I do my sketches."

"I would never repeat such a thing to such a man. He has no confidence in his art. He relies on you to buoy him up, as the shell the ancient terrapin."

"He will need to swim on his own if he wants to be my equal. The carpenter, at least he can float on the surface, in his crude way."

"I am getting less interested in being the messenger of all this."

"Opienne."

"Yes."

"How do you know what is poetry and what is shit."

"The orientation on the page. Poetry generally comes in little boxes with definite horizons. It itself knows what it is. Thus it circles back to itself, knowingly, in rhyme or rhythm or repetition. Shit will spread about like a stain, ramble free. It does not know itself."

"Tell him his poetry does not know itself."

"You don't need to tell him that. But well said. Why so well said? I feel someone else has said it better. Oh yes, it was I, when I told him his poetry was autosexual. I did not put it quite so mildly. The circling back: the sucking of its own . . . but I myself was taking the conceit from somewhere . . . "

Chapter Fifty

Mirra let the phone down and returned to her hammock with more than feigned grace, or grace that knew it was feigned and was infinitesimally transfigured by its knowing. She did not know what she meant by going on about Pearlhorn to Opienne; she often did not know what she meant, she never knew what she meant by anything, and this, said her expression that opened and closed its wings on the Lupine landscape, one less serrated and to her mind more pure than the Two Trees one—this was what Pearlhorn enjoyed most about her, her disarray, her chaos. All possible states of intoxication, including the spiritual foxtrot induced by the Knowem flower, are familiar ground to him, and all forms of solitary euphoria and doom. Add my soul to his, though, and the two, under the cloak of mutual security, push each other into landscapes of wilderness that would never be essayed alone. Easy—it was easy before—we could infect each other with daring—but now that we have crossed the firing coals of this new promise, one that promises to lead to bone-boring euphony and banal bliss, I need service of more. I have many Mirras, I have so many Mirras in me that they can only communicate by bat and whale calls in this watery dark. Eye, moon, grave. From my vantage, from beyond time, no one is dead or alive, the sky is an eye, the moon is a scleratic imperfection. The changes of day to night are my domed cradle.

Lupo was napping on a terrace chaise after lunch of his harvest, chopped and oiled and peppered and washed down with his wine. Even though he lay in shade he wore a hat over his face, to dim out the suggestion of the sun. Without going too far afield I can say that this, to him, was perfect repose, because it is so too to me—the position and the orientation perfect, the sound perfect. The sea battered the land as if it needed just that stretch more of space, as if, if the land were to draw back a stone's throw, the waves would lie down to rest. Mirra dropped into her hammock aslant from him, her head and torso free in the light, her legs swinging below, and she bit into a toleseed cracker topped with liver paste, piece by piece without finishing it.

"For what do you wait,"

she said to his sleeping body. She moved the cracker from her strong to her weak hand, which felt as wrong as anything, as wrong as dropping the cracker on the floor at least, since the weak hand did not feel but only suggested,

"For what do you wait? You wait to die, and to live—both of which, on account of the other, are nothing at all."

The strong hand picked up her brush again and watered it and draped a new set of linens over the broad picture book. It made a motion over the paper that brought into existence forevermore in duplicate Lupo's hatted face—defining the place where the face should be, were it painted on the hat—then hovered the brush over the limbs and core and feathered through the layers of Lupo's discreteness. There was nothing overt in his maladaptation to existence, only the hidden heart, the rest of him was true to the Flavian ratios of the universe, so true that Mirra could paint him with her eyes closed. There, she did it, and there, she did it again, and again and again until the mark of the brush was invisible. The form of Lupo was like one's signature or special symbol at the bottom corner of a far more complex composition—there, she did it again. Opening her eyes, she found that the toleseed cracker had fallen to the stone beneath her; she tossed it to the rackbirds. Representations of Lupo surrounded her; she had even painted one on her bare knee, one on the hem of her dress. She felt tired and spent in spirit. She thought she deserved a rest—or a space of reckoning with her environment without predetermined form. The inspection and worship of a grain of wood could occupy her for years if the motions of day and night (the swing of her cradle) would cease to intervene. She stepped off the terrace and into the field, but here was too much, far too much to behold, and she retreated. A sudden weariness of the skies' immensity preyed on her balance. She kneeled at Lupo's side and matched her temple to his chest. She listened to his heartbeat. Here was indeed his flaw. It did not beat; it rippled and stumbled through time, and sometimes, for longer than she could imagine Lupo surviving, it reposed in silence. Mirra listened, and her hand thumbed through the microclimates that guarded Lupo's existence. It pretended to fix a bruise in the canvas of his skin. It buttoned and unbuttoned a button. And it cringed and fluttered and itched itself over the daydreaming yearning of flesh that distorted the lay of Lupo's skin under the breastbone and fought for life in animate echo to the heart's invisible tries.

"Can I help him?"

Mirra wondered. She pressed upon his belly in counterpoint to his heart's soundings. Her heart pressed from her depths into her ear, and in the center of Mirra's mind the two hearts struck an offbeat chorus. She smiled up at his hatted head, and a tear, now another spread in the rough fabric of his shirt and darkened it. He did not stir.

Lupo was dreaming of a rich meal made of dense fruit and flesh, the fruit pulled from a tree miles high by the arm of a giant, the flesh killed against all odds by a freak accident in the sky that brought down a blue negresorte, a ship-following bird not seen since the time of Juniper Trolley, and the sauce partaking of both, with the addition of something unidentifiable that electrified the palate. The quest for that spice, whose taste was somehow beyond taste, whose name was beyond name, drove him deeper into sleep and conjured images of his first searches: as a student he would roam the capillaries of libraries, places where no one, not even the librarians themselves, had consciously gone, looking for he knew not what, never marking his places, never taking notes, barely remembering, finding total knowledge and total oblivion at once, but for the one line that would stick of its own adhesion (*The Wyndall roundtree is the only member of its family, and it has never had any ancestors nor will it ever be the ancestor of any living being; it is Time capsized*). He would do the same in forests, where he could after many hours of walking and looking know the particular copse and every scent and bole by their real names, none of which could be pronounced but whose sense would flow up and down his spine in washes of incredible color. There was no greater existence.

Chapter Fifty-One

"She is often cryptic, Etienne. Tell me exactly what she said, please."

"This kind of seriousness does not become you. I would suggest you cancel the engagement before I jam this cigarette in your eye. And the possibility of such hysteria must be made notice of beforehand, so a man can take things down."

"I thought she told you to take it down."

"You speak as if I ever care what a woman has to say. I was in the middle of a poem, man. A poem."

"A poem about eating a girl's bottom."

"I'm going to overlook your impolitic confusion of the sacred and profane. And in fact it was the thing right before the bottom. And further, I was on the verge of striking the thing out altogether in favor of something more palatable. It was morning. She broke the spell. That in itself was worth a slap upside the face, if I could have reached through that accursed telephone."

"But her face was not available for the slapping. That left you with narrowed options. You could have slapped yourself across the face, for example."

"All I know is, she did not say she was coming home with any celerity, certainly not tomorrow. You need to trust me, and we need to destroy, I mean enjoy those two little harlots."

"This does not sound good at all."

"Alright. Alright."

" . . . "

"She said your poetry was questionable cum poesia."

"Something I already knew. But how. How questionable."

"She said it did not rhyme."

"Not like her. She does not like rhyme, says it makes the composition seem like an automaton. Circling back on spent symbols."

"Or alternatively that it did not keep a certain meter."

"Only Divos did it with any aplomb. She knows I am no genius. Only a peddler with a degree in peddling and a great deal of anguish. Continue."

" . . . "

"You must have more."

"She said it does not know itself."

"Oh and beautiful."

"I withheld only what I could not understand."

"Never mind, Etienne, this this not your fault. I've fucked myself up with this whole thing. Mirra and mirrors. She's probably just playing some kind of joke on me. Or maybe she wants it for protection. I can't see her . . . no. No."

Pearlhorn walked the terrace in wool slacks dreadfully unfit for the heat. Is this the first time I have mentioned the weather?

The air this evening was pregnant beyond term; the only thing that could relieve one's eyes of their nearsightedness—owing to the placental pressure of the haze—would have been a caesarian section of the sky. Small spurts of relief snuck through the old scars of old bolts of lightning, spurts so transient they mistook themselves for hallucinations. These breezes lingered on the forehead, the manual dorsum, the bridge of the nose in ghostly rumors that mimicked the numbness of approaching disease. Pearlhorn walked the terrace and fumed up grey stillnesses and tipped from a glass of Lilith Four, a vintage that reminded him of all the other instances when he had tipped Lilith Four. This in itself was burdensome. There were the fearful black eyes of a middle-aged Medievalist, who had fallen asleep in half-naked embrace with Aden's brass flacophone. There was a parade on the shore road at Trucula that had popped up out of nowhere and had swept him along to a mediocre performance by a guitarist and his bandana. There was a flatfish meal with frilled haregrass cooked lazily by Ianthe, a week ago. The wine did not have taste to him anymore; he had a mossy groove in his palate down which it glissed, sending upstream naught but the slightly piscine signal that the way was clear for the next guzzle. Pearlhorn had a strong case of Checkered Flag Syndrome. And there would be more checkered flags tonight, in fact he could not see the end of the hallway piked with them, for if he kept one eye to his glass and the other to his cigarette, and still another to Opienne, he kept the last to the stone railing of the terrace where there rested a letter knife and a glass paperweight in which there floated embalmed the wreck of the HMS Batman. He still had the missing hand-cannon's twin, depicting the female Western Flinch, away from display in the desk drawer of a guest room, just for such an eventuality: he could still wage Roulette with his reflection. But the identity and the artifice of the thief bothered him, the fact that she had wished to delay his recognition of the taking, the occasion of the taking, the occasion! Four more dread facts dogged him. For one, when the bakery wall, during negotiations, made its multiple rejections of his proposals, and then belabored its acceptance of Aden's last offer by raising its whole infrastructure and hoofing around the lot in mock thought, it did not seem and certainly did not attempt to note that Mirra, in spite of anything the wall, as agent, might say, had in her possession at that moment the gun, by means of which might be enforced any old rule or scripture of art or life, however inconvenient, including her own suicide. Second, Aden's understanding of conjugal blisses though limited, he now knew that he could not call Mirra back and ask after her orbit and its timing: from a word she would know his intentions even better than he did, and here even he knew that he was headed for the breach. Godwin's. Which brings up, third, Godwin, who, underneath his nerves, underneath even what was under them, in combination with that terrible Scarlet, had him crazed even to the point of not giving a hoot if his heart were diced out of him or his brain fluted into a million grim flotsa, so long as there passed a moment before the fluting in the girl's immediate, closest presence. This was the most childish, and I do not mean young or ill or unformed, but rather the oldest feeling he knew, this desire, the one rooted in his origins, and he originated as a fuck: the feeling was not going to go quietly. The fourth—of course—you can guess the fourth by now—the fourth fact of course was Whitson. Let me tell you something about myself. My ear is not of the perfect tune. There were better poets even walking the earth at the time of Pearlhorn. Pearlhorn was not one of them. Nor was Etienne Opienne, but I would imagine that both could name a better poet. Perhaps Ofal, or Crepe. The latter's "Drum, The Drum of the Drum" had won the Heinous Prize in Poetry twice in one year. The second time was a mistake, suffice it to say I had competition. But there was one place where I had everyone—something I had said first. And curse me, curse Whitson, for having said it.

Any one dropped to earth before me,
And any come after I drop my sandal in
The grave, and whole worlds of moisture
And gravitation in the midst of these
Have no place but mine, they know
Only me. They do not know themselves.
Damned they'll be when I am damned.

Opienne had failed to tell Pearlhorn that Mirra, in her echo of these lines, had been echoing someone more proximate than Whitson, namely Opienne. But even if he had, it wouldn't have made much difference. Pearlhorn had fucked himself up.

Chapter Fifty-Two

Peter hurried toward home to check on his father's progress. He hurried, but he could not arrive yet, he had the strong sense he did not want to know the result of Lynch's ditherings. He took a detour through a middle way between Marywood and Two Trees, through rolls, leans, swamps, hills, hidden views and views poked through with distraction. He parked in a clearing forming a miniature amphitheater for the surrounding trees, a voyeuristic species called Butella's pine, after a naturalist found ensconced face-up in the Carrefor glacier, his glasses still hanging on the nub of his nose and one bushy eyebrow raised in immortal curiosity. At the far end of the amphitheater, a trailhead led through a web of nameless streams. Peter vanished beyond the trailhead and began searching for his solitude.

He found it, lost it, found it, lost it, just as swiftly as the boughs passed. He arrived at a shallow, bug eaten bog over which lounged the whalesome trunk of a fallen tree along whose back he balanced, and he alighted in a pathless forest. The pinch of tickers and the alarmed and alarming calls of rackbirds announced him. He looked around, and knew what it was to look around and know that no one and nothing looked back.

The crowns of trees, lanterns of life, swayed, and their motion drew arcs in him as if carving and re-carving the first clef onto a vast sheet. Inside Peter there formed an ancient chord, a sound without equal in the scale. It was a type of laughter, as if Godwin were standing in the doorway of his mind laughing, making herself naked and the pale pink sky of paradise known on her chest and stomach, and pasting the invisible tokens of victory there, victory over all that troubles the heart of man—feathering herself with the air.

Chapter Fifty-Three

Lynch did not pick up the script again. He spent the day in his chair unable to go to work—what would have been the point?—arms crossed, eyes looking but not seeing or vice versa, the toes of his boots the only noticeable motion, and unable to smoke: he had thrown his Flamingos out the window, thinking the gesture would help smooth things over after having launched a plate in the same direction and blown away the pane. The prospect of cleaning up broken glass had introduced a special weariness, and he now wished that no one had ever suggested to him that he had a way to make it rich. Everything around him suddenly looked worthless. Why were there folds and cracks and ripples in the walls and ceiling? Who had introduced colonies of mold everywhere? The roof, the accursed roof! When he got his cut of the money, he would fix the roof—but why fix the roof, when he could go to the Tremontan coast, leave the entire territory for good, and baste oneself in the waves for ever and ever? Was one million enough to do this? Who even knew? It seemed a bit short. It seemed that, for all the labor and strife he was getting put through, *two* millions would be better than one. Katherine Godwin could afford less: her mother even had a pool boy who swatted away the falling leaves before they met their reflections.

With two millions, Lynch could afford a modest place on the Tremontan coast and a reasonable lifetime whisky endowment, if he stuck to blends. And then, why was he the only one with such thoughts of flight? Was something wrong with him? Why did anyone with the means to fly away to the Jocastas, say, or to the narnic mountains of Roosburn, remain in this island of drowsy souls surrounded by fires and belching smoke and bled by deluge and drought and war and pall? More than this, how could Pearlhorn, having turned dozens of dancers on their bellies and backs in Petrie and Ithico, so Lynch had heard, suffer himself to ninny away his learning and looks on Katherine Godwin? Anyone could tell the girl was malnourished. Lynch would punish the man simply for not skipping town before he went off the deep end of his conscience. Now . . . but he must smoke first. Lynch went outside and around to the glass-strewn endodendron patch and fetched the Flamingos.

"Hello."

"Hello. Mister . . . Pearlhorn please."

"Speaking."

"Good day to you, sir."

"How are you, Peter? Why . . . why do you have an accent?"

"Oh, right. Fine. Fuck. *Fuck…*"

Lynch hung up. Pearlhorn kept talking, but on hearing no response, frowned. Aden had been through these sorts of things plenty of times, more than he could count, but the cuckold involved had never behaved himself so strangely. He waited a moment and dialed back.

"What's going on there, Peter?"

"I thought . . . I thought we could talk."

"That's a fine idea. Let's do it some time. Say next week? I'm a bit tied up at the moment."

"No, I mean talk now."

"Alright, go ahead then."

"I have a problem."

"I can't imagine what that would be. A problem with the property?"

"No, no. The property is . . . fine. I broke a window, but . . . "

"That's your problem."

"I know."

"So is that it?"

"There's this . . . you know . . . I've been hearing things."

"Hearing things. Alright. Have you seen a doctor?"

"No, not things like ghosts. Things like people talking."

"Real people or imaginary people?"

"Real people."

"Is the content of their speech relevant?"

"Real people talking about you in a . . . not so good way. A . . . shameless way, if you'll permit me . . . " (Lynch had shakily, in his delirium, picked up the script again.)

"You mean shameful."

"Maybe."

"I know what you're going to say. So out with it, man!"

"You know I know?"

"I don't know you know, I more figured you didn't and would never know, but so be it."

"Well I do know."

"I'm very proud of you. So what do you want from me? You want me to stop? I won't do that. She is a spirit in need of higher attentions than the rest of the world can offer. I hope you know I mean no insult. So you know, and people talk. Now the real question is, are you going to get out of my way, or do we need to fight over this? Be very careful in which one you choose."

"I was thinking . . . I was thinking I would get in your way."

"So you're giving me notice. What is it you plan to do?"

"I'm not sure yet. I hope I don't have to do it, whatever it is."

"Look. Let's cut the ceremony. You don't seem like you want to make a stink. So let's not make one. I am prepared to atone for my sins, although I admit no sin. I have thought it over already, in fact, just in perhaps a different context."

"Atone . . . If you could . . . explain what you mean."

"Oh come on, Peter, I am prepared to compensate you—both."

"Both? Compensate me? I don't need compensation. It's more like, society, the world needs compensation."

"Society, the world. I've never heard such a thing said about a grown woman."

"Grown woman? She's only a girl. A . . . de-licate, innocent girl."

"A girl? Not to mention delicate or innocent. I don't know where you draw your lines, man, but . . . never mind this, we shall not discuss her . . . I never heard such a thing about such a thing, but maybe you're a Ticker or something. Or a Coot. We haven't really talked religion before, but yes, maybe you're a Coot. But sure. Society, or what's left of it. How much compensation does society need for this?"

"I don't know, exactly."

"You don't know? Alright, I'll bend over backwards and throw out a number. Let me look at what's here . . . this and this and this, and this and this. Funny, I was just going to . . . alright. You ready? You need to promise me something, don't blow it all in one go."

Chapter Fifty-Four

When we left Lupo off last, he lay in his perfect position, while his mind, contained though it may have been within his hat and then again within a dream, sat cross-eyed with scholarly bliss and consternation on a library footstool and tried to decipher the text of a book he could not, no matter how many rotations he gave the covers, turn right side up. Here the book seemed to say that the protagonist, an ancient hero with hilariously exact sword placement, approached the River Hooligan with his army in pursuit of the gory drummer and thumber of the people, Flombery. There were three ways to cross the River Hooligan, and the hero considered them as one considers drawing a set of alternate animals or mythic beings using one constellation. While this was happening, Lupo lost sight of the page, the river, the night sky, lost sight of Flombery and the hero, and considered the question only: what it is to choose between three equal paths, equal in that they carry one to one's destination in the same manner, even the smooth and slippery stones at the bottom of the river the same, even the whirlpools and reflections. He waited for an answer. He waited in the middle of the river for centuries. Civilizations droned and crumbled and railed and bloated and rotted around him. Shamans baptized themselves in the river; the river was diverted and disappeared. Still he waited. The dust and clay of the dry river bed caught the wind, it ensconced him in sunset fury, and he fixed on the lips of his mind the shadow of the taste of exactly that exiled monarch of all that is worthy yet unseen, that viceroy of the darkness. He reached out his mind's tongue to wet his lips. But something interrupted his meditations. He half awakened.

He was still under his hat, and none but he knew his presence there, in the breathy dark. Deep pain in his abdomen approached that of mictural paralysis—this seemed to wake him up entirely, but the half-waking mind is never sure. An arachnoid fussle bothered the off-center axis of his body, the place that should house the machinery of life and death. Or it was more like an avian, a rackbird done perched directly where it shouldn't have, and having a bit of fun riding the quakes that marked out his heartbeats. He waited in delicious waiting for the thing to stop fussling—oh now—oh then, he made a call to his strong arm and coiled it motionless and drew swift back and made with violence for the thing's life and limb.

The motion broadsided Mirra in the face, Mirra who had been hovering nearby, he guessed in order to move that rackbird to equal surprise, which had worked one way or the other. The rackbird had all but vaporized. Mirra moaned into the polished ilewood of the terrace, her head had struck it with the report of a rhonefruit fallen upon the unforgiving root of its mother. He crushed the cap against his face and dragged it earthward and pushing through the fabric a yawning moan in antiphon to Mirra's more strident sounds he staggered over her—he tried to explain—a rackbird was a malicious mongrel of a mocker, bastard murderer of the equinoctial silence—and he tried to help her rise. She did rise, her eyes tearful and dim, her hand full of glowing blood that mixed with the paints on her dress and with the occult designs, it enriched them—she did rise but as Lupo took his shirt off to fashion her a reservoir for all that splendid pigment, she stumbled down the terrace steps as if shot and gathered momentum and all but flew into the tousled heads of the lilith bushes that guarded the balustrade. Lupo chased her with his useless shirt. Things were just beginning to come into focus. A purl of verdant lights came from the north of his vision and left blank sediment where the roofline of the terrace should be (his head was thrown back in anticipation of injury; the brim of his hat, unconsciously flung aside, hung from a lilith branch). It was not safe for an old man to rise so quickly. He passed out of consciousness two or three times, holding up his finger for the gods to wait. There, he was no longer trying, he was helpless, and . . . now he had waxed sufficiently into presence to cradle Mirra's limp neck in his arm and raise her up. A few touches of pigment now showed on his arms—he did not know their names. What he knew was that he should have waited there, by the river in the dream, or reading an upside-down book about a river, or whatever it was, with the constellations swarming about alluringly, and decided, but in dream only, to nourish the river or the book or even the desiccated river bottom with that splash of his hand. The river might have parted, the book might have come truly into being, as a beast sometimes will not act absent abuse. Lupo had problems keeping his sleep discrete. There was one similar occasion to this, on a research trip in the Hyoo-Wut range out West, when he wakelessly rose and caused trouble. Burning up in his tent and stifling himself with the saline lament of his own sweat, he rose and sleepwalked through the camp with his bladder painfully sloshing. Around the fire, seven or ten Natives, his guides, lay prostrate with their minds blown open by hallucinogenics. No one actually saw Lupo emerge from his tent, and when the Natives tried to rekindle the logs in the morning, they found them touched by a rain that had fallen on the fire only (their own bones were bone dry). The Natives named it a foreboding Miracle and spent that morning with their ears to the ground, to hear if the camelmen of the Apocalypse were on their way; one of them shot himself with a poison arrow in anticipation of the Plague. It was Lupo who read the tea leaves: he awakened around noon with a nugget of urine-scented charcoal in his fists, like a tippling cave painter.

Now Lupo lost and regained strained consciousness continuously in the waiting room of the University Hospital at Ex and pretended to read an article on the cleansing properties of dimweed husk in its sun-dried and pulverized form. The powder is known to leech the overage from the liver after 100 uses, and, after ten times that amount, the stray hairs fall from the brain, leaving a fine blank slate ready to be violated again. The doctor came out.

"Lupo Bravo."

"Mr. Bravo, Doctor Theresa Gold."

"Pleasure."

"The pleasure is mine."

"Well, read me the riot act."

"Hematoma and epistaxis. Medium occipital concussive trauma."

"Tell me something coherent."

"She hit her head very hard, Mr. Bravo."

"So much was clear."

"And she keeps asking for a man named . . . Whiston?"

"She is awake! Whitson! Sure. I've got plenty of Whitson at home. No problem. I will supply the Whitson."

"There are other issues, Mr. Bravo. You see, come over here a moment, I do not feel entitled to relate them to you, as you are to some extent the subject of these . . . things, you see."

"Hold up, Doctor. As I understand it there was a bird, a demonic rackbird—I—I was dead asleep!"

"Just a few signs...a few rather serious signs, that your daughter should be held over for testing and possibly further remediation."

"Remediation."

"Remediation."

"Remediation of what?"

"Remediation of whatever we find during testing."

"So you haven't found anything yet."

"We have certain signs of certain somethings that could or should or are probable to be found, which I am not at complete liberty to tell you."

"That sounds like hokum to me."

"I don't really care what it sounds like to you, Sir."

"Let me see her."

"She is not in a condition for visitors."

"I am not a visitor."

"You are, Sir."

" . . . "

" . . . "

"Do I have a say in the matter?"

"This is an issue purely between Ms. Bravo and the Hospital. My apologies for your inconvenience, Sir. We mean no harm."

"How long?"

"How long what?"

"How long!"

"I cannot say."

"Shall I bring her things?"

"You may if you like. Ring for me when you return."

Lupo left the Hospital, and left the medieval university town of Tarne. He drove slow home in his truck, slow with trouble, and slow because tears obscured his way. In storm slanted sheets they flogged everything. Some cars disappeared in air. Lupo nursed the hope that he was living in some sort of symbolic film or dream with uncertain architectural elements, misplaced beds and women, and his parents and their Andalusian college friends peeping in at the wrong moments. But no monster nor twisted landscape of the surreal interrupted his drive. He was alive, unfortunately.

He packed a bag for Mirra out of her childhood closet: a roll of shirts, one dress, a bandana, a pile of mismatched socks, a flannel cape, a gauzelike cape imprinted with moons and stars, scarlet clownish pants ballooning, rusted hapless nail clippers, a pill bottle of aspirin, reining gloves with the fingers cut free, coral blue slippers, a parachute, the gun from where she had buried it, and drove the bag back to the Hospital and called for Theresa Gold. When he returned to Mirra's room, he closed the closet door on himself and droned and underbreathed goads of weep into the smallest corner by the wall, where the cake of years had gathered. His heart rapped panic on the floor. The electric light in the ceiling, already gazing peaked and harrow from atop its tether, blinked at him.

"La primera luz…"

The first lightning of karmic haine was not, as the flounder-shape historian Dooring had predicted, the defense of brother by brother and uncle by uncle (that was the thunder), but the undisclosed goring of the perpetrator's vein by its own proprietor. Dooring had made the mistake of framing the phenomenon as if it were a problem that could be solved. Lupo flew without a frame: the pendulum of karmic haine was the world's one perpetual motion machine, never to be undone. So Lupo's theory ran. It did not help him now.

"I should have written in another language, one which I myself could not understand. I would have relieved myself of the illusion of understanding."

And truly, and truly: I may not live to see another Sunday. Here in the closet dark, in my mind's eye, I see Mirra looking up to the sky at her Sunday self, the one I invented and she denied, but still she looks up at her, so she cannot deny the unadulterated image of her own art, and the two exchange the same gaze, the same I saw when I followed the stones in the floor of Vertico's Cathedral to the final alcove and beheld the statue there. Of that statue, named Mirra by the hand of the Tuleran Master, the expression reaches with parted lips towards an orifice in the wall that is stretched over with glass stained in a vernal pattern—fanlike clouds and filigree of trees. Out there beyond the stained glass, in the cradle of the city, in the dome of the world, there are things and shadows of things that even he, the Master, could not describe even if given an endless string of lifetimes. And even once described fully, if such were a word, those things would change again, within themselves or without, and be once again beyond Mirra's and the Master's reach. Add to this, that the Tuleran Mirra, frozen in awe, cannot, but for on a rare day when the light neutralizes the image on the glass, even see through to the mystery that lies outside.

Chapter Fifty-Five

"Why does it need to move, Scarlet?"

"To torture us. There is no enticement without torture."

"But that is a negative argument, and the sun, see how it reaches into the sky with wanting. I can't climb any further to slow it down."

"It doesn't care what you can and cannot do."

Katherine Godwin and Scarlet May had secluded themselves in the paxwood tree with equal hope that their elevation would inspire the sun to illumine them forever. Godwin had grappled her way to the dawn of the tree, the first figure to cast shade, the etiolated wisp of life that gave last definition to the air above. She reached up and caught and returned the gold dust that shone from the edge of the world. The dividing line of day and night hovered past her fingers, she reached higher, and it faded off her again. The sun finished playing to its amphitheater and bowed deeply, touched its nose to the ground and raised its skirts flamboyantly behind, and that was all. Godwin looked down. All below her was scrambled, you could not see the void, and Scarlet lay on a bed of juniferous needles and paxwood arms that received her and rocked her. The strands of hair that fingered forth from her temples and fell behind her in array left what Godwin mistook for smoky impressions of Scarlet's mind on the lower dark. Katherine swung in arcs that seemed to traverse miles. Here was the campanile of the Dimwielder's palace, and there it disappeared, and sometimes she felt she could kiss the stone of its sides, but just as promptly it would recline into the wilderness of her mind. Here were the bone glints of shields and swords of wrecked and smoldering armies and wafts of dour carnage from the fields, and there the seas of kill receded into motes of turnfruit and asterid pollen, unguent scents brought aloft by the summer evening mists. Godwin teased her cheek against the mast of the tree and closed her eyes. For a precious time there was no motion and there was no fear.

"Katherine."

" . . . "

"Katherine!"

"Scarlet."

"Let's go down."

They went down, and Godwin was weakened with gravity as she approached the earth. On the last limb she hovered and shook, and Scarlet needed to pull her down by the ankles. The two fell together, rose together.

"Scarlet."

"Katherine."

"I was up there."

"Yes."

"And I thought I could stay up there for many years. Maybe even—a hundred years."

"You could stay up there for generations, millenia. We could all crucify you and then ask you for favors, stupid little things like pay raises. How would you like that?"

"I would like that a lot. That is my entire tend in this whole thing. Godliness."

"What whole thing?"

"This whole thing. I don't have any other name for it. I want to be left alone at the pinnacle of the known universe, where not even I can breathe, and where blood pours out of my brain to let go the pressure—there, there is my connection. I want to suffocate, to squander, to have my blood rust on my belly and to make it my skin. I—I have a confession, Scarlet. Can you—can you first give me a bit of that?"

"It's strong."

"I know it's strong. It will be my only strength, this drink. Baby, baby. You don't know what I'm about to say, do you? You think I'm in love, don't you? You think I would kill for this one— that this whole thing is a mask. Don't you?"

"I do think you are a fool, if that's what you're asking."

"That's because you're in love with everything. Your voice itself cannot but cling to the very core of the being. You reach out, I reach in."

"There's no difference, Katherine."

"Oh there is. I bleed inwardly, or around and around, but I want to bleed out. I eat, but I cannot hold, I must expel, I must give forth. And no amount is enough—I hollow myself to the bottom, and yet still there is more. It reminds me of those lines:

I spent my life in search of what / I knew I could not find. By definition it is beyond my reach: I want to know what it is to die, to tell of it."

"You should drink more. You underestimate the power of drink."

"God damn it, is that all?"

"Or give it back to me—at least I can appreciate it. And we should go to them right now. Pearlhorn and the poet, what's his name."

"Restraint! We need to prepare."

"Restraint. Mine was lost many years ago, to a curtain rod. What, does yours regenerate each week?"

"A have a feeling Scarlet."

"I have a feeling too."

"All might not have been lost, if I had stayed in that tree."

"All has been lost for a very long time."

Chapter Fifty-Six

Two Trees, the estate not the municipality, has two main entrances, front and rear, and three more, dirt or dirty, to the appurtenances—ruins of the original farmhouse, ruins of the stables and slaughterhouse, an overgrown airstrip, a shattered aviary, an herparium, the gardener's cottage, and the garden. The gardener's cottage and the main allée of the garden were built as far apart as possible, for in the eyes of the famous landscape architect Buoy Ralston there should be no gardeners ordinarily visible in the garden, no traces of their rinds nor pipe tamp in the grass, no peat smoke on the Baron's horizon. The garden, not a garden at all really, for there were no paved paths, no artificial ponds, no fruit trees, few flowers but for the guarded and sparse Stagger's Rose, traced a full arc around the perimeter of the property if you walked it a certain way; it traced a star or a figure-eight if you walked it differently. You could also trace and retrace the stalk of an exclamation point, but why one would want to do so was beyond Buoy (and thus he had a sign installed on one of the less weepy evelyntrees that read "DO NOT TURN BACK"). The outer arc was not Pearlhorn's favorite and rarely walked—somehow the idea of a perimeter bothered him, and he tended to walk the drive, whose roadbed was of finely crushed stone, then take a zigzag path through the dometree thicket back to the house; so when Opienne insisted on taking the long way to the Lynchs', better to enjoy the sundown and better to catch sight of duskmoths on the wing, Aden advised boots: the outer arc, tamped by naught but time for the past many years, would be full of false floors. They suited up in the cloakroom. Reclining on a lacing bench with his laces splayed open, Pearlhorn tilted his book to face the half-open window, made of a scene from the famous Fallopian Hunt in which the Jester offers an urn of fish to the Prior. The book was one whose words Pearlhorn could only take a few at a time, or he would be glutted to paralysis. Whitson's *On Summer's Last Eve.*

> *Who knows the dawn better than I, who*
> *Always misses it in dreams, lacking alas*
> *The eye for light, the eye for you, the eye*
> *For us—cast by opulent blindness toward*
> *Black cliffs glistening in spray, black*
> *Canyons overborne by the deep, canyons*
> *Where dreams, themselves, sleep, where*
> *The dawn is a faded fingerprint of the dawn.*

I often indulged in repetition, for fear of venturing beyond the strophe into that realm where nothing was certain—and the result was a kind of herded joy. So Pearlhorn thought. He closed the book—the one poem had sapped what energy there may have been to turn the page—stood, did not care to lace his boots, grabbed Etienne, burst into the fields and the air already heady with the headlong weight of night—and shoved the volume into his back pocket. He could have left the book behind on the bench, but he would never find it again; whole cities, continents had been lost to him that way. He could have put it in the laden duffle bag he had with him, but then he feared he would leave too rich a gift at the gardener's cottage. While he could reproduce a dollar bill, he could not reproduce his marginalia. Sometimes he thought he wrote things down to forget them; this thought was as indulgent a fictional ritual as his marginalia itself, for unhappily there is no forgetting of any thing. There may be lapsed recognition, a line or a face that enters the consciousness too steeply, an angle at which everyone is a lover or one's tormentor, and fails to raise her true flag before the beholder is enraptured and scared to death at once. Thus did the face of Scarlet May—Aden and Etienne were just passing the foreboding fingerpost joined to the admittedly overweeping evelyntree at the last reach of the crepuscule's light and the allée; and their conversation had turned to pure banter in the vein of their early friendship—thus did the face of Scarlet May, trucking towards them in a kettle-sized Lesso by one of the three auxiliary drives (from the gardener's cottage) and kicking up phantoms of stone dust, with Katherine whooping and hollering beside her (they had run into an optimistic Lynch), enter Pearlhorn's senses with a fearsome foretaste. Pearlhorn flinched. The girls pulled alongside the garden path, at a natural bend in the road where it was possible to gaze up the tongue of the park to the mansion that glowed in its throat. No no, not here, Aden said—continue, continue to the house and wait there. And he began to feel the fact of his connection with the earth question itself.

Chapter Fifty-Seven

"Please speak clearly, or we will have to repeat the process."

"Why must I speak?"

"You are not forced to speak. But you have been speaking, and so far as you will speak, please make your mouth movements heard."

"That is disingenuous. If I do not speak, I must remain here."

"That does not necessarily equal a must, Tierra. You may remain here as long as you please."

"Mirra. Mirra!"

"What does it matter?"

Mirra was propped up on a mountain of pillows under a baroque canopy at the focal point of a lecture hall at the University of Ex. Having visited Ex with her son just weeks ago, she recognized through the hall's cathedral windows the University's trademark jagged archways embellished with Saturnine creatures, the ivy that grew like winter beards on the northern faces of its buildings, its tulip trees impossibly tall, and the proximity and special motion of its air. She lay naked on the pillows, unmoving from the wiry nodes stuck to her breasts, her brain, her fluttering stomach, and her ankles, and from the thick needles that drew her astonishingly plentiful blood from one arm into the circuits of a maze of tubing that ran in desultory, deep purple arcs and deposited it into the other arm. Both networks, electric and fluid, clocked in at a light post from which the masked Theresa Gold took readings. Things looked worrisome from the look in Theresa's eyes, her only visible flesh except for the flash of the orilan that fluttered out from behind her smock when she turned around. The benches in the hall were full of academics who had flocked in like bifocaled geese since Mirra was wheeled over from the Hospital. I, Whitson, watched from the wall, my back against a replica of the Tuleran Master's *Child and Mother*, my crown against the child's feet, whose toes were spread like ferns. Filling the whole vaulted space, when it did speak, was Theresa Gold's voice.

"Let us please start again then."

"You can't possibly . . . "

"You say he was your father."

"Is. Is my father."

"But his identity, says the test, is that of a piscine fossil found in Fife, four thousand years old, that now reposes in the British Museum. In other words, we have drawn a blank as to your heritage."

"He is not such an old man. He is say, I should say, not much older than I am, in geologic time. Just old enough to make me. He made me."

"Can you explain for the audience how you came into the world?"

"I embraced it. I embraced my family, though it was not the family I would have wanted."

"When?"

"In the beginning. And since then all too seldom. It is a difficult thing."

"What is difficult?"

"Adoration of anything or anyone is difficult. Far more difficult than you all seem to recognize."

"Adoration of a fossil is hardly of a world. A fossil is, in fact, if you'll permit me some artistic license, a death mask."

"I is I. Call me what you like, I think my head is better now, my head is all but glorious, my life-mask is now intact, I would like to go home."

"Oh you're going to love this."

"What?"

"Sorry, I thought I had muted myself. Now. Home, you say. Getting to the point, Tierra. Where is home?"

"Two Trees—Lupine—Please unhook me if you're going to heckle me here prone and naked like a slave. I cannot cry with these needles pulling on my veins."

"What municipality, what nation, Tora? What exact place on earth are you from? Can you find it on this map?"

Professor Gold spread a gigantic map of the World on an easel in view of Mirra and the majority of the crowd, and she handed Mirra a long wooden pointer. Mirra could not move to manipulate the stick, much less tense to hold it steady, for each of her arms was punctured by a needle. She dropped the pointer on the floor.

"It looks all fucked up."

"Tora, it is absolutely accurate."

"I have never seen such a thing. Nothing in nature is so edgy. I would start, perhaps, with a cloud, and if there were no clouds, which is hard to imagine, I would nonetheless invent at least one little floater, for depth. I see not a single cloud in this picture."

"Imagine it was a cloudless day when the cartographer undertook his craft. Now describe to me, since you cannot point," (general laughter) "where it was *on this map* that you issued from."

The light post flashed green, red, yellow, green, red, yellow. Now white.

" . . . "

"Mirra."

" . . . "

"Mirra!"

Mirra awoke in the hospital bed. Theresa Gold smiled.

"Do you feel my hand?"

"I think so."

"Can you follow the light? Not. So. Good."

Theresa walked to the foot of the bed and palpated Mirra's feet. She pinched her hard on the calf ("Yike!"). She pressed lightly on her stomach.

"Your scans came back fragile. I'm giving you a prescription for the pain. You will have trouble accomplishing things.

Reading. Doing household tasks. Working. Sleeping. Do not drive. You will be sensitive to light."

"What am I doing here?"

"You were struck. You fell. Your father knew well enough to take you here, and not the Lupine infirmary. I recognized your father, the famous historian, he writes on . . . what does he write on again?"

"Everything."

"You are still not good. You will not see so well out of that eye for some time. The swelling will go down. Would you like me to take you home? My day is done. I seem to know where you live. Two Trees, I see here on your chart. It rings the wrong kind of bell that I cannot place."

" . . . "

"Home, do you want me to take you home?"

"Lupo."

"You would need to do that of your own accord. I am already breaking the rules."

"Home then."

Theresa Gold and Mirra Bravo got into Theresa's Hermitage. The Hermitage, back when it was made, took the last Gordian King and Queen on their fateful cruise through the streets of Hemingway and Rife-on-Tune: their blood stuck to the velvet like frosting. Leaving Ex, Mirra Bravo's cheek rubbed the blood purple lap of the bench seat clay grey and back again.

"Why does Two Trees ring the wrong kind of bell, Doctor Gold?"

Theresa laughed a humming laugh, she was not quite sure, she had been so fucked up that her memory was blind. She did not recognize any of the dark sights on the way to Two Trees. She did not recognize the feeling or flow of the road. She did not recognize Mirra from the portrait on the Lynch landing, nor from Peter Junior's eyes, whose color could be mistaken for their mimicry of Peter Senior's black Irish, but were in fact descendants of Mirra's Spanish Spanish. She did not . . . she did not know why she felt so strange. She felt as Mirra must feel: beat up. But Mirra was asleep on the velvet seat, and her tiny body was of an indestructible beauty. Theresa peeked at herself in the rearview, her eyeliner had begun to escape its bounds, she looked like a tired whore. The pillars of Pearlhorn's estate passed in the rearview's background. The electric massage of the gravel woke Mirra.

"Two Trees," said Theresa. "I get a horrible feeling and at the same time a wonderful feeling about this place."

"Drive to the top," said Mirra.

Chapter Fifty-Eight

Earlier in the evening, the meeting between Peter Senior and Pearlhorn went off even warmly: neither man knew what the other was buying, and Pearlhorn handed over a bag stuffed with millions in cash—meaningless to him and earth shattering to the other, whose lineage, through generations of impoverishment, in all senses of the word, had never seen anything so titillating. Pearlhorn opened the bag and shone a powerful Ronson light on the bounty, a flourish that caused Lynch to leap from the couch and hit the ceiling, he could not help himself, and to wake his son who was napping from the slack limbs Scarlet had caused him earlier. When Aden walked back outside, Etienne Opienne was waiting, smoking, swatting at cacophones and shaking his head.

Peter Junior had been dreaming of a phantom landscape where the light was always that ecstatic low-angle light that comes just as the sun breaches the horizon—on the way down or on the way up he could not tell. There was a rambling paneled and candelabraed house full of people, and they were all just nearly fucking. Playing with each other. No one ever climaxed in his dreams, his imagination was like an orchestra that could not find its cymbalist. Was it because he always closed his eyes when he came? Was there a way to keep them open? In the corner of the glowing mansion had lain a girl with the most mysterious face, one he had not met before but knew with his soul from eternity. He plunged himself back into the dream.

Downstairs, Lynch could not focus, he was mesmerized with riches. Five or ten or ninety lifetimes—he could not contain himself—likely lay in the bag, he didn't know, he could not bring himself to put a number on a lifetime. He would wait—yes—wait and drink himself hooting drunk, until Peter Junior awoke, then he would sally out to buy a mountain of cocaine. He guzzled down what remained of his cabinet, he took a lap around the house (Poor Harry! But now all was redeemed!), he fussled with his fly and attempted to milk the tension behind a tree. It wouldn't go, wouldn't even reach out to meet him. Very well, he capitulated (to what?), he would have another peek, just a small peek at the prize that would endow his future. Forget that girl, he couldn't even remember Godwin's name right now, he and the kid would make a run for it, maybe leave a token million for the idiot girl's bright thought. Alright now. Get your head together, Lynch. Get your head together. Understand to whom is owing the prize. Call down your son.

"Kid!"

" . . . "

"Kid!"

"What."

"You need to see this."

The girl murmured something having to do with whales. She moved the dream Peter's hand between her legs, then squeezed it so hard that he could hear his bones shatter.

"Kid!"

He left his hand lying dead in the girl's thighs and descended the dark stair to find his father babbling to himself in the terrible tones of an orilan having inadvertently caught a sea urchin in its beak. Lynch did not notice his son; he walked past him and into the kitchen and shook an empty bottle over his glass.

"There! There!"

Lynch shouted far too wildly, and indicated the bag that lay wrapped up far too neatly in its folds and zippers, as if Lynch had fondled it into the shape of something else on purpose. Not able to restrain a smile, he felt he had not smiled such a smile in far too long, Peter approached, and he opened the bag along its major seam. But what? But what. There was some wrapping to be gotten through. Old newspapers showing the dirty doings of others, grey, purple, sky blue, pitch black. Perhaps a wry nod to the red background of the situation, as Godwin would put it (blackmails showed scarlet) . . . now he dug further. There was considerable weight to the thing, there must be some golden core . . . Peter looked around. His father was breaking bottles maniacally against the crux of the sink, one after the other. Peter scattered the papers wide and far, he plunged into the very center, where a ponderous box needed a knife or some such . . . he danced round the fading vision of his father and retrieved one, and blazed into the final sanctum.

"..."

A beautiful piece of machinery waited there, inlaid with the design of a bird of paradise, so Peter thought. So—fine, the man did not have so much cash on hand, that was understandable, at such short notice—this seemed as worthy a treasure as any. There was a handwritten note attached, perhaps confirming authenticity. He lit its face with a flame. Where had that flame come from?

What I would give to you could not do better than this. It fires true. I regret that one shot was all I had left. You can get more ammunition at Furling's, if you miss. Up through the soft flesh of the chin is best.

Yours,

Whitson

Peter looked around the room. Everything was shivering and making as if to get up and leave out an imaginary door. The light, the paxwood clock, the walls and even the darkness were gathering their coats in the cloakroom. The sear in the carpet left by the match he had lit was crawling towards the exit; the man in the kitchen was trying his best to become a memory; the broken glass was climbing the hills of echo. Peter looked down at his hand where the gun should be, and that, too, was turning into a symbol of death, the shape of an inverted question mark made by his index finger and thumb, to rest at his side until the time came. He took one last listen of the forest creatures as their harp strings frayed, and finding that simple moment enough, he made as if to pull the imaginary trigger against the tender undercarriage of his mouth.

"Boom!"

He cried, and he, too, dissolved into the night.

"Kid!"

Now Peter awakened in earnest. Awakened, and he swatted duskmoths that were whizzing around him and invading the sheets, huge birdlike moths with painted faces on their backs. Lynch seemed to have a truckload of these creatures, and was flinging them at Peter with joyous abandon.

"We are going out kid, you and me."

"That is a shitty idea. Unless you mean to put all this in the bank."

"The Casino, kid. I'm going to turn this into a trillion dollars."

Chapter Fifty-Nine

Pearlhorn and Opienne started back up the hill, now in half-mooned and porous darkness, and at a clip that threatened double but pulled back from the upper pace for fear of drawing some extraneous curse.

"I somehow knew they would come early."

"I would have appreciated some notice of your knowing. I stink like a bordel from my own thoughts. And one other thing."

"And what other thing."

"You just paid for something you already have. That man's wife, you've had her a thousand times, I would guess, conservatively. Now these two, each half her age, what beautiful symmetry, safely contained in your castle, and you with command of the gate—that I would pay for."

"All we do is pay for are things we already own. Birth, death, and the middle matter, the reading material, so to speak. Where is my Whitson? Here he is. If I get through the night without losing this book, I will consider it a day well done."

"Humility, virtue, poise. All come to you with two nubile whores in your driveway. I'm not surprised."

"I'm sober, is all. Let's see what happens when I'm not."

They ascended the final headland and crossed with authority the gravel courtyard, as if to attend a convocation of nations. The two girls were leaning against the still boiling Lesso and waiting and chainsmoking Sics by the two, themselves still afraid of cutglass abandonment even at this late and long fatidized and all but airtight chapter of the tale. Before the men appeared in the gaslight of the drive, Godwin, all but choked up with nerves and constantly taking tips from the whiskey bottle and checking herself to make sure her moonblood had not arrived early and unannounced, had even given away her prize:

"I love you. Take him from me, before I lose myself entirely. I will have Shut, or Open, or whatever his name is. I hate his poetry—but I hate Pearlhorn's even more—I can't even read it—I imagine it was all written to me."

"And perhaps it all is. I would even say, if you believe so, it is so. You are the saint and the devil of his poetry. And therefore his life. But only for now . . . "

"And he—if I had poetry in me at all—he would be mine. But that is just my overruling objection to all this, that at the height of adoration acted out, at the joining of the saint and the devil in one body, in the possessing, at that very narrow summit, with wind and lee to the sides and no lack of sunlight, I know that my body will not wish to descend. To continue."

"If you would pass that thing back to me . . . don't guzzle the entire bottle, you'll have nothing else to go on but a dreg of sanity . . . if you would allow me a thin bright line in your veil of despair, what is so wrong with descent?"

The men approached; the girls approached, and in swift sequence offered the bottle, their mouths, their bodies, or was it the reverse. The moon and night birds and crescent luciferous evening bugs made way. The night made way. Godwin approached Pearlhorn, she stank strong of the luxuriant sap of pax, she touched his arm. Feeling, even knowing that he could not move now without a guide, she pulled him through his own house, to this room and that one, opened bottles and cupboards and closets and stairwells and false corridors and even tried to open false doors that led to false places, all the while whispering in a ridiculous tone,

"The deal is, you will fuck me, and then you will kill me. You will drive me to untimely death."

" . . . "

"Fuck me then kill me, and you will have me. Or do not fuck me. That is the deal."

" . . . "

"I had a reason, I forgot the reason, I had one and lost one, I am beyond reason, I am back to my beginning,"

and not at all minding his confounded silence, and not at all seeming to hear, when he and she found the perfect place (outside on a bird's terrace off a forgotten servant's room on the third floor facing the sleeping Painted Mesa), where the corpulent air alternately enfolded them and shily heaved by averting its eye, she stopped, and he said,

"For the sake of the gods let me have a drink. And stop talking all this nonsense."

She shared some of what she had swept up in her arms. There was no Lilith Four, unfortunately. A full fifth of Armannleger Vintage, two bottles of cheap Cape Verde Cabernet, a bottle of Tawdry Port . . . Over nips and swallows of this and that, they had some conversation. Pearlhorn could not make out what he and she were saying, he could not believe that Godwin was sentient, he was shattered. Godwin's power over him was so strong, the emanation of her sex so acute that with each feathered movement of her thighs, his heart was given a stinging, incurable paper cut. There was no pretense in her gaze: she was hooting and raving mad for Aden Pearlhorn, and before he could wonder too hard how it would feel inside her body—what sorts of unexpected twists and textures he would find there—he had disappeared inside of her—once, twice, and then over and over again, he disappeared and reappeared again. She didn't kiss him, didn't get undressed, it was done with the flick of a finger against the button of his pants and the expert placement of the cock under her skirt, as if she knew it from a former life or had learned about it in school and repeated the movement by rote a thousand times. Then there was the total submersion, total extraction bit that she executed without flaw perhaps a thousand times, and all the things she was saying—it was very nearly fiction, the way she repeated back to him verbatim his own internal narrative of their parallel lives from the beginning and interspersed it with little ecstatic apostrophes nearly of pain—except he could not have fictionalized such an all-inclusive sensation of being, and would not have let himself go so quickly and secretly. He prayed he would not go instantly dead, but Godwin's youth that had carried him hence carried him a few miles further. He lost sensation for an instant, and just as quickly gained it back.

"That afternoon with the heat I was on the garden bench and I asked you what is the meaning of Anna's suicide and you told me that question is worth no more than what is the meaning of trains. And the sense I had of your ironic nihilism and the worship of all things as worth an infinite amount of value . . . looping around and meeting at the bottom of the wheel like sugar and salt or communism and monarchy and that look you gave me and the thought of you taking me into the woods where we take each other *Yes no no no Yes no no* in the afternoons made my whole body electrify itself and I soaked the back of my dress laying there and you had no idea what you were doing, your face was so nonchalant and brilliant I could have cut you open and crawled inside just then. Hold it right there now yes now . . . God I'm so close. I think I'm afraid to come."

He tried, but she was. She let loose a few more sloppy flourishes then stopped.

"Try touching yourself."

"That's cheating!"

"Then I'll touch you."

"Ai! Too sensitive."

"Then I think what we need is a breather."

"You still haven't answered, I think that's why."

"We will all die in good time. Let's go see what the others are doing."

Pearlhorn put a polished and ardor-flecked and mostly numb broken curtain rod back in his pants: Now what? They began to descend towards the common rooms. Scarlet and Opienne could be heard laughing far away. Was it the kitchen? No, but the kitchen had clearly been scavenged. A loaf of hard bread and a bent and fat-caked salami and a jar of mustard seemed highly disappointed at their fates. Where was Ianthe? Still *gone*? It would have been aesthetically bracing to weave her into this final scene, Aden thought. She wouldn't talk so much, for heaven's sake. And her proper conscience would have led her to cook up something fortifying before everyone made way for the breach. Poor Ianthe. Had she flown back to Switzerland? What was wrong with him, anyhow, always trading the ones for the others, and the others were infallibly labile as armies of lady Napoleons—and the ones were always so perfect? Aden escaped Godwin's vapor trail (why was he following her around his own house?) and ducked into the pantry for a bottle of Lilith Four. The pantry was cavernous, it even had its own wallpaper: ducks and Indians, and wounded ducks. His mother Nore used to shut herself up in it when her time of reckoning with the proximity of toxic overkill would come. Her chair, an uncomfortable interpretation of a chair, still sat, unamused and cross-legged, in the corner under a miniature gilt-framed etching of two fairly worried fish. A tentacled ashtray lorded over an even more min-iature table. Unfortunately, the pantry did not seem to have a corkscrew (while we have been surveying the part of the pan-try not occupied by shelves of preserved foodstuffs, Aden has been frantically searching for a way to open the bottle of Lilith Four without emerging). Aden could see just through the nar-row opening in the pantry door and past the Romanesque and Moorish vestibule the smile of the wing of one of those silver saviors on the kitchen counter, next to a slaughtered array of vintages. Godwin's voice was heard sweeping the corridors, frantic too, among the triumphant cries of Opienne and Scarlet that issued from all parts.

"Aden where? You where? I need you, Aden, where did you go? Please do not leave me, here in this place, here in this late hour. Did you fall asleep? Did you get lost? I am the lost one Aden, please, I am the lost one, please. You know who I am, the same that you know from before life began, I am your deliver-ance and you do not want to be delivered—I am the echo of your soul—and you, and you are the echo of mine, we are as songs found just floating on the breeze, birdsongs and such, treesongs, songs of . . . ."

He pushed in the cork and closed himself in the pantry. Lilith Four spurted everywhere. In the dark he found Nore's chair and the ashtray, just delightful. He wished his mother were not dead.

"I don't know why you would do this Aden, I told you, you should have killed me, now you have not killed me but I wish I were dead, this is the only possible result, to wish one were dead, because I am falling headlong back into the fear and monotony of my life, and you are nowhere to be found, I will not recognize you anymore, only as an icon burning up in my hearth for some last warmth. Kill me! Kill me. Show yourself and murder this last husk of Katherine—her name is not even Katherine, her name is unspeakable. Are you, where are you? This is not an accident, is it? Fuck you Aden, fuck you! I could care less if you died of a massive injunctive anginal coronary catastrophe. And fuck the apostasic gods you worship like their little cock slave. Fuck Ralston and Keith, fuck Turner and Ommergung and Josfrende and all those Baroque fairies of art. And more than ever fuck Whitson. If you are listening, you cowardly thieving wretch of a poet, Whitson, I'll see you in Hell—"

(Pearlhorn emerged, in Lilith Four smoke.)

"Now calm down, little girl. You don't have to go that far. I was just trying to find us some passable wine, although you'd better not have any until you've aired out a while. Come on, let's see what the others are up to."

Chapter Sixty

In the afterlife, Lupo could not sleep that night. He indulged in visions that all this suffering and divestment was fake, that he would wake up the next morning to Mirra at her orlanfruit champagne on the terrace, fragile face with cautious yet affectionate expression, apologies waved away on the salt wind, apologies for aping a bird on his chest, apologies for imagining a bird on his chest, and a deep hollow nothing in his mind told him that morning would not be. He had a ballooned lip from biting it raw—this made his entire body feel deformed in comparison—and he heard a voice telling him he would die again from that very self-inflicted wound. In his histories, especially those where his protagonists were eternally at war with one another, he was obsessed with finding the point where a character, or a man, became invested with the knowledge of the hour of his death, and was not wrong. A drab exactitude, but the final. There were birth dates and death dates, both set in stone from where Lupo sat, and something happened to all men once they knew the latter for sure, did not just think they knew it, but did know it: they began to live. Lupo took himself out to the dunes of the underworld. The landscape was heavily animate. Other beings, headless birds, brown poles and terrygraphs and broken and desperate souls saw the morning where there was none, and wore themselves out shouting at it such that when the first light did come, they had already died again from exhaustion. People collapsed and dissolved where they stood, and got up and began shouting again, but their shouts were not shouts at all but bursts of color that turned to ignominious halos of fire that consumed them. The sunrise itself was the impossible rise of a silence over a melody where the melody kept playing but the silence played too. The fiction's tension built up in Lupo's brain, and he felt it leaking out of his ears in disbelief. Lupo let his mind fork and flow out of his skull, what else could he do? He reached out for the chaos, and was born into death again.

Chapter Sixty-One

Meantime, at the "high spinner" roulette table in The Socratian, champagne bottles litter the floor. Peter and Peter are down to their last pair of prostitutes, a Pomerican and her sister, little dark beauties in skyscraping heels with firm shiny buttocks like wet volcanic sand. Some of the others, breathing hard, fingering their earrings wide as haloes and their bosoms stuffed with cash, are standing at a distance, wondering if they will be asked back upstairs as part of the round robin grand finale. People place their bets. Here comes the pitch. No more bets. The ball slides and rolls and skips and settles. Thirty three. Peter and Peter tilt their blasted vision about the board searching for the thirty three. Nothing. But nothing ventured, nothing gained. They place their bets again. What bets? Where? Peter Junior turns to his father and asks, where is that one chip that I told you to keep in your pocket, in case we lost it all? Where? Where? Oh no. No no no no no. Ladies, excuse us. Ladies excuse us. They take the interminable elevator to the highest floor of the hotel, where their suite lies in ruins. The bag, slaughtered on the table, is empty. They look at themselves (in the copious mirrors) and they look at each other. There is one thing left to do.

"We kill ourselves."

"We go home, kid. We go home."

Father and son descended to the parking lot and drove away. The Socratian disappeared under the hills. In between curses flung with waning passion into the smoky cab of Lynch's truck, the two seemed to agree that the money was meaningless, that the things it bought were no better than the ones they already had. And that Theresa Gold, despite her eccentricities and imperfections, was more valuable than all the whores in the Socratian piled together and propped up on a thousand pillows in appropriate positions. Yet when Lynch and his truck seemed reticent to pull off the main Two Trees drive towards the family cottage, when a devilish smirk arose on his face similar to the one he showed himself when he pissed in the sink, when he suggested that the two of them would have nothing to lose by testing the whole material riches hypothesis again, Peter didn't fight him. They, too, drove to the top.

Chapter Sixty-Two

Mirra walked in the front door of Two Trees with a bewildered Theresa Gold at her side and thought that this would be the moment, to a sane mind, where the protagonist should beg the gods to take her back. The voices of two young and familiar girls and two older and more familiar men filled the house from the far end of the gallery. They were loud and their sense was intelligible.

"I need to get fucked up," said Theresa.

"Go ahead,"

said Mirra, and she stood in the foyer alone. Up there, he slipped on a numis stair and hung like a deposed monarch from the banister. He whispered to himself, I could hear it, no more of this. He did whisper. What did he mean. No more of me, or no more of this? Or did he mean no more of life? Do any of these statements have meaning? Can we ever end something? This hand cannon. (She dug in her bag for the gun and put it in her mouth.) Can it end me? My god it turns me on, it makes me shiver. I want it. I want to feel and to know nothing, to become the inanimate earth, and to wait for the rains to wash me away into the sea, wait for the clouds to pick me up, wait for the stars to ripple out of the sky and swing down to kiss me. I want to be free. I want to forget that I knew myself. But the only freedom I know, I will experience without sentience. It will not seem like freedom, for I will have forgotten . . . it will seem like a greater and even more terminal captivity, to be down on the riverbed, or up in the sky. This, this is all I have. It is gruesome up close, it is splendid from a distance, like the sun. Why can I not get closer? What am I afraid of? What use is fear?

Lynch's truck roared into the courtyard, and its slipstream shook Scarlet's Lesso. Gravel exploded against the house. Theresa Gold asked from the kitchen where was the wine.

"I don't know. Ask Ianthe. Where is Ianthe?"

Mirra walked down the gallery towards the commotion. She stopped at the door to the study, where she was still unseen. A liquor cabinet was nearby, through fault in design. She took a pull of something. It botched all her traincars, sank her in the familiar quicksand. Now. She listened. Opienne bleated in French, her high school learning could not capture the elegance of his entreaties, but he seemed to be egging someone on, every now and then he cried, putain! and putain! and pu*tain*! Aden was silent, he held his breath until suffocation brought him near paralysis and he gasped like a castaway washed up on the beaches of—Santa Theresa. Scarlet May delivered in a hoarse whisper critical commands to all concerned, she was the Starbuck, Stubb and Flask of this ship of fucks, her body and the body of Katherine Godwin were being manipulated against threat of certain hanging from the spanker boom of anyone who demurred. And Godwin (Mirra took another pull, and another), in halting and starting half-whimpering melodies and sidenotes and footnotes, was telling a story. Mirra could not follow the content, but from the inflections of Godwin's voice she could tell that the story had a beginning, a middle, and an end—and that Godwin knew them all. The story's pauses were seasoned by the chorus, by Aden's forced breathing, and by Godwin's claim that she was so close. At these points all hands would turn the chorus up a notch, until it was clear that Godwin had missed her chance. And around and around again. And around again. The girl was never going to get there, but the chorus was not giving up. Peter and Peter paraded into the kitchen and found Theresa Gold. Mirra took the bottle of whatever she was drinking and walked into the room.

Godwin's screams came first, everyone stopped moving, and then Godwin did come. She ejected herself from the tangle of limbs and off the couch, where she bundled herself in a fetal position on the floor and screamed a newborn howl and choked herself with laughter. Opienne made himself even more unintelligible than before, he seemed to be yelling in Old Church Slavonic. Aden walked away into the narnic alcove where his chair and lamp waited for him. There was no Whitson draped over the arm of the chair. Where had he left his book? Scarlet slipped the gun from Mirra's hand and laid it down on the mantle and pulled at Mirra's bottle and her clothes and her body.

My characters lost control of themselves and their purpose, lost gravity and reality and faith and need for faith. Time careened off a cliff into the waves. Theresa found a treasure trove of Lilith Four in the basement and took up Nore's scarf from the sipping chair and tied it around her head, so that when she danced, late on into the night, in a drawing room heaped with bottles and bodies, with Lynch and Opienne to Aden's pristine record of Carol Mima playing the Songs of June, it seemed the two men were dancing with a giant blue bird. Aden was drawn out of his shame by the sight of Mirra carrying Godwin outside and down the terrace and into the fields, where she laid her down and whispered, the love of my love is my love, and the three were scathed and seared by the grass until they could not be parsed from the landscape. Scarlet and Peter, paralyzed by each other, matched hand to hand and foot to foot like the moon laying over the sun and breathed into each other's chests the words, over and over, we will never die, because I will never die from you and you will never die from me.